ETERNAL NIGHT AT THE NATURE MUSEUM

SARABANDE BOOKS *Louisville, KY*

ETERNAL NIGHT AT THE NATURE MUSEUM

STORIES

TYLER BARTON

Publisher's Cataloging-In-Publication Data
(Prepared by The Donohue Group, Inc.)

Names: Barton, Tyler, author.
Title: Eternal night at the nature museum : stories / Tyler Barton.
Description: Louisville, Kentucky: Sarabande Books, 2021
Identifiers: ISBN 9781946448842 (paperback) | ISBN 9781946448859 (e-book)
Subjects: LCSH: Home—Fiction. | Loss (Psychology)—Fiction.
Loneliness—Fiction. | United States—Social conditions—Fiction.
LCGFT: Short stories.
Classification: LCC PS3602.A8426 E84 2021 (print)
LCC PS3602.A8426 (e-book)
DDC 813/.6—dc23

Cover and interior design by Alban Fischer.
Printed in Canada.
This book is printed on acid-free paper.
Sarabande Books is a nonprofit literary organization.

This project is supported in part by an award from the National Endowment
for the Arts. The Kentucky Arts Council, the state arts agency,
supports Sarabande Books with state tax dollars and federal
funding from the National Endowment for the Arts.

CONTENTS

I like feeling at home, but I wish I didn't feel it here.

—MARY ROBISON, "In Jewel"

ONCE NOTHING, TWICE SHATTER

Luther buys cars. It's what he does, and it's what his billboard says he does—LUTHER BUYS CARS. He bought my dad's car. He bought the mayor's car. He came to a surprise party for my mom's sixty-fifth and left with her Sportage. Think back. If you lived in Gettysburg in the late aughts, Luther probably bought your car. Maybe you heard about him on TV, about what he built, and you thought, *I would never sell that man my car.* I'm sorry. I don't believe it. It's his aura—smile like the grill of a Chrysler, hair a horse's mane. Luther glowed gold.

I was en route to leaving town, to finding peace, to ridding my life of so much *me*, when I crashed into the back of an Integra, transfixed by the riddle of its vanity plate—HEDIE4U. My brakes tried. Our cars veered into the cornfield. The other driver's baby cried as we waited for the police, and it was raining, pouring, and my door wouldn't open, and Luther appeared, bearing an umbrella and a guarantee: my Buick was totaled. Bereft. Unsound. With his big vocab, that quiet murmur, the cleft-lip scar, you just hung on to Luther's every word. I was cold, high, and scared, but his serenity kept me from fleeing deep into the corn. Luther went *shhh*, and then he bought my Buick. "I'm notarized," he said, and shook my hand with both of his—so warm. "It's all legitimate."

I left my eleven books on Zen in the trunk, took my hamper, and walked to Wawa. I bought so much made-to-order—enough to kill a

꠴

horse, as they say. "Mozzarella sticks for pumps two through eight," I told the cashier, sopping. Luther had made me magnanimous. I thought it was my middle-aged life turning over like an antique engine. That night I got a nose ring. Not that Luther was pierced, but his high-tier moxie made the world feel like something you could bring to heel.

Luther bought my car for three hundred dollars, but then I had nowhere to live.

After the accident, I stopped wearing the hat a fan had made me, a red mesh trucker embroidered with the words *Brad the Broadcast Bandit*. It'd been two years since my shock-jock radio show, and I'd been going by a slew of dumb identities—Greg, Jed, Art, Hal—any name that sounded burped. Todd. I started living in the yard behind my dealer's double-wide. Basically it was a doomsday shelter dug by shovel and lined with ten-pound bags of rice. That's where I slept, on rice bag beds. I cut this guy's grass, loaded his little dishwasher on wheels, and kept his cats alive. His name was—I'll call him Colt. I owed Colt a lot of money, and he had dirt on me too.

"Don't just do something," Colt would say. "Sit there." Which meant: *Do something*. And then he'd hop on one of his crotch rockets and tear off into the afternoon. While he was out, I'd clean his trailer, and I'd clean his girlfriend's trailer; I'd clean his other girlfriend's trailer, and I'd clean her girlfriend's trailer. I thought about a billboard that said, TODD CLEANS TRAILERS. At first I figured I might get empty this way, cleaning all day alone. What I wanted was to make my ego go quiet, to learn to think of nothing but the dish when I rinsed it. But then one morning with the radio on, I got lost in my head and snapped a porcelain plate. Then I smashed a glass. Then I whipped the squawking radio at a ceiling fan and left.

So I tried Mom again, walked all the way to her house, offered to cook and clean for a spot on the couch. She lived in an unaffordable split-level that would soon be repossessed because the loans had been written in a language the country no longer spoke. In '09, that was the story of Adams County, the elegy of the country, really—homes being pulled out from under us like rugs.

Mom raised honeybees and wasn't fond of taking off her aerated beekeeping veil. She looked like an outer space nun. Through the mesh, she told me my problem was that I didn't know how to blame myself for anything. I had to start doing right.

"But I don't want to do anything," I said. "That's the point. I want to want nothing."

"You hearing this?" she said, turning to her hives. "You see what I'm talking about?" I told her I was becoming a wandering monk. I threatened to join the US Army. I gave her a hug.

"What about that nice man Luther?" she said. "I hear he's hiring guys like you."

Cars, yes, but it turns out Luther had also bought land, so much land, enough land to kill a horse. In May, trucks drove over to spread dirt into an oval, a track. That's why he bought our cars—to stock a demolition derby. Even miles away, in town, you could hear vehicles collapsing into one another, and that's when I came to Luther for a job, holding my hands out like a cup, empty.

Piles of busted rubber tires fenced the track, and I entered slowly, passing teams of men wrenching Jeeps with gusto. In his shed I sat on a red fender and told Luther to make me a driver, a derbyman, a dead-to-the-world heel on the gas. With enough impact, I'd smash the grasping clean out of my body like a pair of dumb dice through a shattered windshield. Luther rocked in his racing seat, prayer hands pressed to his marked lip, eyes shut in one long blink. He wore a white tank top you could see his dog tag necklace through. I poked at an eraser on the table between us. There wasn't one light on, but the toolshed shone.

Finally he said, "Todd, you consume drugs, correct?"

"What can I say?" I twisted my nose ring, smelling the sour of my cartilage. "Youth."

We laughed at that. I was forty. The hole was infected.

"Substances deliver you a kind of . . . orgasm, yes?" Luther said, every word a whisper.

I shrugged and did not say: Yes, they used to, they once helped me see all the way to god. "Todd, the goal is to be in a state of perpetual," he said, pointing to his temple, "orgasm." I laughed. "And that's why we're creating the Track."

When he handed me a paper, I thought it was his manifesto. He told me to read aloud:

> Anybody know what this place is? This is Gettysburg. This is where they fought the Battle of Gettysburg. Fifty thousand men died right here, fightin' the same fight that we're still fightin' amongst ourselves today. This green field painted red, bubblin' with the blood of young boys. Smoke and hot lead pourin' right through their bodies. Listen to their souls. I killed my brother with malice in my heart. Hatred destroyed my family. Listen, take a lesson from the dead.

For a second, I felt heroic. I couldn't put my finger on the film the words were from, but it felt like one where when people fall down, they keep getting back up and keep getting back up.

"I'll employ you as my anchorman," Luther said. "You'll narrate the races. Remind the crowd precisely why they're here, why they want to return." I shook my head no. Airtime was the one drug I could not do anymore. If you're listening to this, you know I've relapsed.

Remember the Titans. That was the movie. And Luther—a titan. Tycoon. A tyrant-to-be. I heard people outside the shed laughing, saws coughing into metal. Luther stood up from his cockpit, came around the table, and put his hands on my shoulders. I shivered, but it felt holy.

"Can't I just clean the dirt?"

"You've got to be somebody before you can be nobody," he said, pulling an I-9 from a glove compartment nailed to the wall. Had he been reading my old mystic books? In his words I heard Thich Nhat Hanh and bits of *Be Here Now*—ideas rang familiar but newly bold, glossy, like chrome. Luther handed me the form. I read it aloud, but Luther wouldn't laugh until I signed.

Luther tore tickets. Luther sang the anthem. Luther sold snacks. Luther mopped the johns. Luther meditated alone. And for these reasons, he didn't watch the derbies. And because he couldn't watch, it was important to him that the story I told through the loudspeaker rocked. I used a voice other than my natural and hid in a booth made from the detached cab of a Durango. With my microphone and my Diet Mountain Dew, I said everything I saw.

The Excursion is, oh boy, turning, gunning, and the Civic doesn't know it, but he's about to get a RUDE wake-up. And on *rude*, the cars crashed. Mud flew. Every once in a while, something came on fire. I popped addies to keep my focus, E to get the crowd excited. I narrated from the perspectives of the cars everyone loved. Your Avalanches, Chargers, Colorados, and Broncos—anything sounding ripped from the West. They whooped and booed at my command.

I couldn't help it, becoming someone again. My ego ate up every noise they made.

There goes Crown Vic, America's hero! The crowd would erupt. *Lick 'em good, Vic!*

One night Luther motioned for me to roll down the window and handed me a thesaurus. I started using *careen, incognito, tragicomedy.* I said *indigent* and *aroused.*

Admit it: when Punch Bug surrenders to the barrel roll, you feel a UNIQUE arousal.

And on *unique* my crowd would tear a hole through the air.

Sometimes when a part fell off a car, I'd declare a dance-off, and anyone in the audience who wanted that bumper or that mirror or that broken, melting helmet would stand up on the bleacher and shake it. Our camera guy would shoot slow across the rows until I found a dancer I couldn't criticize. The winner got to run out on the track and pick a prize.

In the parking lot, after all was smashed and done, Luther would gather lingering fans for a last beer, gratis, and do what Luther did best. Often he'd stand on the cooler. He'd whip out this statistic I think he made up, about the average Pennsylvanian spending three hundred hours driving every year. "Each of these precious minutes is spent on a road that's designed to take them exactly where they've been told to go. You comprehend?" Forceful but breezy was the way he spoke. "We've forgotten that we can color outside the lines." Some listeners would stay on, join up. Our crew grew large.

There's no denying how magnetizing it was to see your own car out there on the Track, broken and totaled but—my god—firing back up again. How the motor always, eventually, turned over. Within a month, we started running double features, Sunday specials. Eventually, Luther lent me a car, not to smash, but to use. It was a Celica, which means cosmic. I backed it up into all of Colt's motorcycles on the day I left his place for good.

One night in July, I found Luther behind the bleachers, swinging a sledge at a wrecked RAV4.

"Boss?"

"Go ahead and clock out, Todd." Luther swung underhanded at the front tire, and the hammer bounced from his hands. He sat in the dirt and nursed his wrist. "Meaning *farewell*."

"Mind if I take a swing?" I said, not wanting to leave. Luther shrugged.

I swung. I swung, and in a minute it was obvious that all we want is to be young again.

Luther watched me lay into the windshield—once, nothing; twice, shatter—and then asked if I would hold a second. He climbed into the back of the car and sat still in the middle seat. Legs crossed applesauce, he held his hands together at his chest. Luther let his eyelids close.

"Use the vehicle," Luther said. "Perform your tantra, the physicality of enlightenment." And I heaved the hammer up, a slow arc, and brought it down like a house. The back bumper cracked and a cloud of spiders poured out. Like a hangnail, that bumper hung on until I slammed it again. I swung until the thing was in pieces. Until the make and the model and the year disappeared. These were things that didn't matter anymore: the make, the model, the year, the future, the past. Things like what we know. What mattered was the place you built to go inside your head. What mattered was your sanctuary. Not what was coming down all around you.

"But remember, it is only a vehicle," he said. "Never become dependent on your vessel."

My knees buckled when the Toyota looked like gum, chewed.

Luther's aura glowed louder than ever. The ceiling liner drooped down around his shoulders. A tear in the upholstery made it look like the car had swallowed his skull. I got in and sat passenger—we meditated together. You could hear the moon. Time got loose.

"What is the first of the five Yamas of Yoga?" Luther whispered. He didn't wait because I didn't know. "It is ahimsa, or nonkilling. Then nonstealing, nonjealousy, continence . . . and?"

The last was truthfulness.

Luther made money, so much money, but he only seemed as happy as the guy on top of a consolation trophy—always smiling with his teeth tight. My pay was decent, and I hardly protested when Colt came weekly to collect half my dough. I just gave it over like always.

You have to remember, I was trying so hard not to want anything. I helped the food crew with their gardens and tried to practice detachment: if the tomatoes ripened they ripened, and if they rotted they rotted. Some were stolen in the night, and I failed; I cared. What Luther preached was the abdication of attachment. No more clinging. I gave his weekly speeches to the crew. *You must detach from your sense of morality. Without bad there is no good; all good creates all bad. There is no hippie without a cop. The goal here is to start sensing all phenomena as one—no good, no evil, just is.*

Luther, my boss. Luther, something else. I didn't want to let him down, so I helped him transform the Track into a compound. We made bleachers from bench seats, captain's chairs, the railing cobbled together with pipes. A bus chassis became the foundation for a bunkhouse, though Luther used the term *dormitory*. Dozens of us worked 24/7. On shelves made of mangled doors, Luther built a library of Eastern thought, and it featured all my old books.

In a month, we had a kind of halfway home built out of

automobiles. I wasn't the only one who started sleeping there. Drivers boarded too, taking turns cooking eggs for breakfast. I'd try to get them talking about their jobs, about how it felt to destroy the body you were trapped inside. "Do you ever get the urge to take the helmet off?" I tried. But they ignored me. Maybe they hated my affinity with Luther, our intimacy, the way he touched my head during meditation? Maybe it had to do with Colt coming by and taking my money every Friday. Our security team made me meet him on the street, and as I handed over the money, you could hear them spitting. They called me *Told*, as in *Does what he's told*.

Luther, they loved. He'd given their lives purpose—kindhearted ex-cons, crabby old men, stupid kids addicted to pills and Monster Energy, women who'd left the shelter forever. They would follow him into battle, me high up on my horse with the bullhorn, calling out Luther's messages to our rabid audiences: *How many of you lost a home? The government and the bankers—they gambled away our lives! The Track is a home. Let go of what you're grasping for, what's always slipping through your fingers. Show us you're ready, sell us your car, join us tonight!*

One night, during our weekly RAV4 session, a schoolteacher who'd quit her job to work at the Track came by with a question about using chunks of rubber in the children's play area. I was cloaked in sweat from hammering the car, and Luther's head was lost inside the drooping upholstery.

She looked shaky when she said: "Just want confirmation from you before we—"

"Excuse me," Luther yelled into the Toyota's ceiling. "Did you observe the two of us before you approached?" She winced. "Never interrupt when Todd and I are fellowshipping!"

It wasn't like him to yell. The woman left, ignoring my wave good-bye. I remember thinking: Wait, we have a children's play area? I tried to clear my head, resume concentration, but Luther's hand grabbed my shoulder: "Who's the man who takes your money each week?"

"Who?"

"The one who comes every Friday on a motorcycle. Who steals your pay and leaves."

"Oh, he's just someone I owe."

"The only one you owe is you," he said. "Tell me the truth. What have you hidden?"

The thing with Colt was kind of a shakedown. The drug debts were done, but he had a video of me from a few years back, full throttle on a mix of pills, stealing a Shetland pony from the mounted police unit at Jefferson Carnival. Officers on horses, if you can believe it. One cop had his kid there, holding the reins of this short shaggy horse, posed beside a sign that said BE SOMEBODY! During some chaos with the Gravitron, I snuck the little horse into a field and fed it tomatoes, just so many tomatoes, and by morning it died.

Colt had been there, filming, because we filmed everything back then. We thought we belonged on TV. Earlier in my life, Colt had been a wild friend who raised my temperature, plus my supplier—the means for my journey to anywhere but Gettysburg. But the day after the pony's death, I told Colt I was done for good, and what he did was send the video to my bosses at the radio station. Now that I had left him for the Track, I knew he'd show the cops if I gave him a reason, if I stopped paying. I had a record for possession already. Theft from the cops, the murder of a horse—I could never handle prison. The word for all this was extortion, I think.

"You're under remote control," Luther said, eyes closed, his cleft scar trembling.

"Nah, it's just nothing. I'm not attached to it."

"Brother Todd," Luther whispered. "You can't let something go until it's gone."

Next weekend, Luther unleashed a new special event: DOUBLE-WIDE DEMOLITION. In the center of the track, a ramp made of recycled metal led to the front door of a local sap's mobile home. Luther had given the guy ten large, a gig as a greeter, and a bunk in the dorm, which everyone was now calling a *barracks*. From the stands, the old man waved at the camera. The engines ignited. Every single onlooker lost it, screaming. You could hear us from space.

Ladies and gentlemen, I said. *Prepare yourselves.* But I didn't know what for. I was terrified. *Because I think we're about to cross a line!*

And on *line*, the Crown Vic wrecking-balled through the wall. The owner had left his pictures up, his bookshelves full. The ruined pages caught up in the dust like leaves.

That night, we had a team meeting. Drivers, grounds and food crew, construction, visitor experience, recruitment—all of us. Luther bowed, waved, smiled, and then handed me a script.

*Tonight we embark on a groundbreaking drive. We're bringing the demolition to the customer. In order to release them from their material lives, we will erase their homes. We will be the Amazon-dot-com of carnage. This customer has paid handsomely, and we need the funds to complete the transformation of this dirt lot into the temple we deserve. I need five drivers—*and here, the hands went up, just so many hands—*you're going to the Viewbridge Trailer Park off Lincoln Highway, Lot 21. There is one rule, which is to make the place rubble.*

I couldn't comprehend the words I'd been fed, but the address was familiar. Soon, five drivers had their engines revving. I found Luther at the RAV4 and handed him my questions, each one boiling down to *Why?* and *What is this?* I passed the barracks and wondered why exactly we needed a barracks. Colt. It was Colt's address. Don't just do something. Sit there.

"Your drug dealer is stealing from the whole community," Luther said, his head in the roof. "Do you want to waste your life being hustled, or do you want to locate peace?"

"I don't want to hurt anyone," I said. "You know . . . ahimsa?"

"Pain, pleasure—feelings are only chemicals," he said. "It's all the same thing: nothing. And, relax. Colt is not presently inside his domicile." A muffled noise came from the trunk. I'd given Luther my car, my man-hours, my voice. For all that happened at the Track, I was guilty.

And I still am, listeners—don't forgive me.

"Brother Todd, I understand. Colt was once your vehicle to enlightenment, and his drugs showed you, for a brief moment, the light," Luther said. "Let all of that go. The light is inside."

In the dirt I found the sledgehammer and put it through the back window. Screams came from the trunk. "I quit," I said. "I want to leave. I'm leaving."

Luther called a car, and in a minute, a Volkswagen was idling beside me. When I got in, the driver—a woman wearing a welding mask—locked the doors. I didn't know where to tell her to take me, and I felt relieved when she chose the direction. Luther did not wave goodbye.

Minutes later, there I was, sitting shotgun in a Golf, ten headlights beaming on the home I used to clean. We were a spacecraft that, as the engines revved, was about to ascend. I didn't try to stop it. That night, I only used my voice to scream. An old woman in curlers watched us from a next-door window, shaking her head. We passed through Colt's weak walls like a gale force, the plastic siding and plywood shattering around us. I heard cats howl. The radio was on inside. When we reached the backyard what we did was reverse.

Colt stopped coming by the Track on Fridays. I didn't know what happened to him. I still don't.

By the end of August, we had a mess hall, fitness center, studios where artists made mosaics from the shards. My mom, newly evicted, kept the gardens stocked with pollinators. There was a position here for anyone. We shipped in red clay for the derby surface because dirt slowed you down. Under the new halogen lights, the slick adobe shined. Turnouts skyrocketed, standing room only. The Track was like a university, an outpost on the moon—the dust of crushed glass embedded in the clay and made everywhere we walked look like a Kingdom.

But it started to feel like a jail to me. I took long worried walks past our blooming gardens, through the junkyard, Brothers and Sisters watching and whispering in their own earthy language. Yes, there were issues with trust. To use my car, I had to ask Luther for gas, so I stopped driving. Nobody talked to me. Even Luther was a cold shoulder. Nights I could hear him fellowshipping with others, the sound of hammers on metal ringing through my sleep. I went to the library, looking for guidance, but the only book left was Sun Tzu's *Art of War*.

I still narrated the derbies, though poorly. I rooted for and preached about the inner lives of the cars the crowd hated, the ones they booed—the black Bonneville, the knock-off Oscar Mayer hot dog bus that couldn't turn, the pink VW bug doing donuts in the back. *Don't trust anyone, Punch Bug. Believe in your true essence!* Crowds, kids, members of our hundred-person staff would come to the window of my booth and beat the glass. The cars went at each other like bulls, and I was hoarse-throated and high, yelling: *Any place you stand at all you are vulnerable! Truly, there is nowhere to stand! To make it out of this ring, you must find a way to be formless! Oh no, the bus is gunning it. Here she comes. Unless you've found a way to disconnect your mind from your physical body, folks, this one's going to hurt even you fuckers up in the nosebleeds!*

The night of my last derby, the Crown Vic, fan favorite, was destroying everyone. Vic could take all manner of damage—windows busted, roof caved, bumpers barely holding on. Painted like one of those rocket popsicles, smashed like a stepped-on flag, I called the Vic French just to spite the audience. The only other car left on the track was the much-hated, all-black Pontiac #0.

Long live number zero! You're an old soul and misunderstood! Our beautiful audience, listen to me: Go home. This is not healthy!

And the crowd chanted back: *LO-SER, LO-SER, CRUSH HIM, PO-LICE CRUIS-ER.*

More like, Le Cruisiér, I yelled into the microphone. *You French fuck!*

The cars raced, and the packed stands turned feral. Luther came to my window. I refused to roll it down. He berated me through the glass, asked who the hell I thought I was.

"If you want to leave, Lieutenant Todd," he said, "there's the fucking door!" But he was pointing to his forehead. And bleeding from the nose. Out on the track, the car chase ended when #0 finally drove through the black rubber boundary and escaped, but the hero still needed someone to hit. Luther signaled like a coach. Fifty yards away, Crown Vic turned toward me.

Yes, I said into the mic. *Do it.*

Vic came, pedal down, straight for my booth. I watched it coming.

You're still listening, so I imagine you want to know what I saw: I saw America take her helmet off.

Here comes a pancake! I narrated, gripping the dashboard. *Or should I say CRÊPE!?*

And on *crêpe*, the cop car came through the gate like a fist, but I rolled out of the booth before it went up and over, slamming down on its ceiling, my Diet Mountain Dew all over the fractured glass. Unscathed, I looked out at the crowd, their faces elated, bewildered, mouths agape, children crying, the moon above our whole scene doubled-over with laughter. Luther vanished into the crowd of bystanders. The Vic did donuts in front of the concession stands. I saw nothing sacred, no one I trusted. I heard nothing truthful. Then I saw the #0 abandoned in the corner of the ring, which is where I ran, screaming.

The #0 started right away, but the thing was, it didn't turn left. Fans pointed and yelled as I drove in circles past the stands. When the gate opened up to let Crown Vic loose on me, and the roar of the stands reached tsunami levels, I gunned it for the exit and crashed through the gate door, knocking down half the pit crew. But I was out. I maneuvered right through the parking lot toward the exit, a break in the wall of tires. The engine rattled like a mob of neighbors knocking at your door. Above me: a hole in the ceiling I could see the stars through. The road opened, but there was still this feeling of being trapped, and I thought of Luther's theory about how we only go where past roads lead, but when I saw the sign for Route 30, the Pennsylvania highway that's rumored to run all the way to California, a sense of freedom filled me, and I chose it, but it was a left-hand exit, so the car kept going straight—straight through a red light, down an embankment, and end over end. My heart fell into my head, totaled my brain. Have you ever felt your karma clear? I thought I would have zeroed out. Things broke I didn't know could break when the car landed on its windshield, obliterating the dash, raining debris—but I wasn't free of anything.

At the police station, they asked me questions, and I asked for help.

"I think I'm in a cult," I said, and the room was silent. "But I still feel alone."

Detective Ulrich explained everything they already had on me—the horse, the trailer I helped demolish (the neighbor lady had ID'd me), the reckless driving, the drug possession. Apparently, she had sent a pair of officers down to the Track recently to investigate Colt's disappearance, but they ended up selling their cars and quitting the force. Ulrich wanted me to wear a wire. Here it was, another cycle. Again I asked the question I still ask to this day: Will I ever escape a microphone? She patted my hand with hers, and if I'd been the old Todd, I might have fallen in love, followed her to war, but no, I didn't trust her. Trust for people does not exist in me anymore, regardless of the fact that we are all waves breaking on the same shore. Her voice sounded as if it had fallen into a well, like she was speaking through a straw. I kept slipping into some space between awake and sleep, and she interpreted that as me nodding yes.

Not all heroes wear capes. This I know because Luther had started wearing one. I found him the next night out behind the bleachers, lying facedown on the hood of a Focus. At first I thought it was a red blanket draped across his back. For that second he seemed dead, my order to trick some confession out of him now pointless, the tiny microphone taped to my chest just a moot joke.

"Luther," I said. "Captain."

"Lieutenant Brother Todd," he said, still as a statue, cheek squished against the windshield. "I have a new job for you." His voice was smoothing out, like he was about to buy something of mine. But I had nothing left to sell, so I rushed into what I'd come to ask.

"Do you remember my friend Colt?" I said, sticking to the script Ulrich had given me. The car groaned as Luther rose, the red cloth Velcroed around his bulging neck. He looked dead. "*Friend*?" he said. He took hold of my shoulders and looked me in the eyes, his pupils almost nonexistent. "You know what I saw in the Middle East, Todd? Bedlam. Chaos. Even our regiments, our own commanders, inept. I've been listening to the Tao on audiobook, and you know what I hear? It's chaos all the way down. If nothing exists, then there's sure as hell no order. The bank took my fucking house, and I thought I had nothing. The house my father built was no longer mine. But now? Now I have a sanctuary. As do you, Brother! And the government is worried that we found it! They're watching us, Todd! I'm seeing things, things I don't like!"

"Are we going to be attacking any more homes?" I said, enunciating.

"Brother." He touched my head. "I never had a friend like you. Will you do me a favor?"

His boot was untied, and I swear, some part of me tried to kneel down and knot it.

"Please," he said. "Get into the back of the Focus." My legs shook as I stood my ground, but Luther grabbed me by the nose ring, pulled me to the trunk. Inside, I tucked into the fetal position as he slammed the door. "Knock once if you want salvation," Luther said. "Twice if you need hell." And for what felt like all the years I had been alive, hail the size of hammerheads fell. The loud was so powerful that I could hear my own soul squeaking. I tucked my nose down into the collar of my T-shirt and whispered, *Luther buys cars. Luther buys cars.* But the codeword wasn't working, because I didn't hear sirens. All I heard was Luther's sledgehammer falling hard against the trunk, the metal pinching down like teeth, pinning me in. Have you ever tried to picture all the people who love you standing shoulder to shoulder in a field? It was just an empty field. Where was Ulrich? Couldn't she hear me? Listen: don't forgive me. Don't feed tomatoes to horses. Only be someone if you have a reason. Is anyone listening to this? Colt and I wept together burying that animal. Man, if you're hearing this somehow, email me, we'll have you on, dude, we'll let you tell it. I say *we* as if it isn't just me alone in this studio. Jesus, I hate this part.

From inside that tiny trunk, I could hear the engines of derby cars, their backfires, the footsteps from our hundred-person crew. The whole Track crept close through the quiet night. It was dark in the trunk, but light poured in when the backseat dropped forward and Luther handed me a mic. I accepted it. His script was simple, a long apology, a rant in which I begged forgiveness.

"Anybody know what this place is?" I whispered my final address. "This is Gettysburg." And when I got to the part about the field bubbling red with the blood of brothers, I went off script and tried my best to give the police reasons to swarm. "We're going out tonight in cars. We will demo downtown until it is rubble. Sword Store. Gun Depot. Wine and Spirits. We're going to meet back here and wait for the rest of town to arrive. They might bring guns, but we'll show them what to point them at. The world. The rest. The country. They might bring pitchforks, but we'll put them to work in the fields. If they bring torches, we'll cook s'mores. If they bring dogs, we'll have pets." I wondered if I was the only one who could hear the sirens.

"We built something here, a new way of living," I said, giving it every ounce of personhood I had left. "Put your hand up if Luther bought your car. Now close your eyes. Keep that hand raised if you would sell it again."

THE SKINS

The producer wanted wet hands. Sweaty and tense to where the sound really snapped. So my team detained the clappers in an overwarm anteroom beside the recording booth. Made them wait. Clammy, anxious, beating on the soundproof door—*We're still in here!* Eventually they were released, palms moist, only to find their mark at the mic and fail her. Each time, the producer sighed. The perfect clap was somewhere far off but—she assured my team and I—reachable.

She wanted trim nails. Short fingers. "I need *compact* percussion." At noon she called the bassist's handclap *languorous*. "I need hands that don't take all day to come together." We brought in children, but they had no strength. We brought in brawny wrestlers, varsity but rhythmless—and even though I could've made it match the beat in post, the producer wanted someone with an intuition she could sense. A soul she could hear on tape.

She wanted my team to stop bickering. A chat about the proper pop filter had spiraled into a dispute over whether, in a finger snap, the sound was in the friction between thumb and middle finger, or rather in the finger's striking the palm. Battle lines were drawn, mapping neatly onto two worldviews, neither of which the producer was interested in exploring. An intern was let go.

ᔰ

"What if you just do the clap yourself?" I asked her, trying to distract from the episode. "We'd probably have it in like one take." But this song was a part of her Selfless series, records with pages and pages of credits. *One is only built from a pile of others,* read the pull quote from her *Vibe* interview, even though the album art was always, front and back, full-bleed headshots of the producer's stoic pout.

"No, Ziegler." She loved to put a touch of Dutch on the pronunciation of my name, even though I had never stepped foot in Europe. She had her own engineer in every country, refused to fly me out for tour. "It is not my role to clap," she said, pressing the delete key to erase an entire track.

So I brought in music students who cupped their hands in exotic ways. It didn't take. We got creative, idiotic—we had a policeman fire a gun. Blanks, but still. "It sounds forced," she said. One by one, my team began to flee, talking of union contracts, families, the sour taste left over from the finger-snap debacle. "It's getting dark," they said. "Outside, too."

Hours meant nothing. What were hours? The coming lump sum would float my team through another summer. The payday was out there somewhere, invisible but within grasp. Marcus and I had decided not to adopt until I was established, until my name was a stock you could trade.

"You're getting all their information, right?" she asked from inside her stress-relieving VR headset. "The failures, I mean. I need each one credited." Yes, I assured her, and then made more calls. Calls. Calls until my phone died. I wandered down the street, past the café, past the poke bowl place, past the new lofts, and into the barber school. They didn't seem to understand my request, but I left an address. One man set down his scissors and shook my hand.

The producer ate dinner—a family-size bag of peanut M&Ms—right there at the soundboard. She'd suck the candy down to its furrowed core, pinch the nut from her tongue, and stack each one beside the mixer. It was times like these that I'd try to break a clipboard with my hands. I'm still working on it. Perfection, to me, is a pile of trying. The pile grows high enough to be enough. "You know, Ziegler," she said, "I'm not paying you for an opinion." And before I could sulk away to send some emails, she softened, turned to me, and confessed that perfection was immortal. "Omnipotent, yet quotidian," she said. "Like finding a dropped dollar."

"More like a million of them, all at once."

Our only agreement was that the handclap is the supreme snare. No drum, acoustic or digital, sounds immaculate as that: two hands brought together. To this day, I get a little kick any time someone calls a set of drums *the skins*.

When the barbers arrived, the producer was sugar-crashed on the couch, facedown, so I led the session—instructing them through the microphone. "Just clap," I said, forgetting to hit record, and the four men began to applaud. My team was gone, so I cracked up all alone. My laughter woke the producer, who stood and leaned over the board, watching as they kept clapping.

"Who are these men?"

"Barbers," I said.

She touched the red button to capture their ovation. "They work

with their hands," she said, raising her arms above her head—a
victory, a stretch.

The song, you'll notice, is totally snareless. No claps, no snaps. No
pillars prop up its structure. It marks the start of her Formless phase.
You can hear a thread throughout, soft in the background—applause
like rain. If you scroll through the credits, you'll find me buried there,
beneath a sea of names.

IOWA DARTER

Friends, you only ever wanted to know why.

Hands against the glass, you demanded reasons, motivations, explanations, plans.

It happened in the Wild Pond Life exhibit at the Mason-Dixon Young Learners Museum, on the morning the tilapia trapped an Iowa darter in its mouth, backward. Remember how the tilapia swam with a tailfin peeking from its lips? Friends asked, "What's wrong with that fish?" Always there was something wrong. Always there were questions. And always, on Sundays, there was this man, Ed—his tag reading *Edwin, Playworker*—standing in a cloud of your unanswerable mysteries, surrounded by the silent ghosts of the museum's dozen other dead fish. Victims of bad PH levels, infrequent feedings, or the mean food chain. "How is it breathing? When did this happen?" The animals, his employment, your endless questions—it all made Ed's hands shake.

But there was one question you were not asking, a question so terrifying that you didn't even know you wanted it asked—*how does it feel to be eaten by your own kind?*

It was Ed's fault. You'd been climbing in the Tree of Forts when he called through the funnel of the Talk Tube—"Any friends wanna see a fish inside another fish?"

Ed: his gruff smile, his anxious movements, the tattoos that peeked from his collar when a top button came undone. Imagine him there by the tank, congratulating himself for being entertaining, for remembering to call you *friends* instead of *kids* or *hey* or, on bad days, *what?*

Four of you gathered at the tank in the Ag Lab, watching the tilapia swim like nothing strange. Either the darter was still trying to swim, or the tilapia was still trying to swallow. The big fish wore a slight frown, the darter's tailfin waving in its mouth like the low flag of some lost country. That wispy tail fluttered, tickling its nose. Do fishes have noses? Ed didn't know. He surveyed the small crowd of you and asked, "What do you see, dudes?" But he meant, *friends.*

One of you: "Looks like spaghetti hanging from his mouth."

Another, whining: "Lemme see!"

Then you with your glasses pressed to the tank: "Monster. Kill it. Get it away!"

And last, Darth Vader, in your dark armor, slick gloves, long cape, wheezing through a black plastic mask: "You save fish?"

It was Sunday morning and, friends, the museum was slow. Across the street, in the high school soccer field, a marching band rehearsed. Their metronome knocked through the Ag Lab's open window like a persistent, unwanted neighbor. It was time, tapping away, as the darter remained trapped. Ed thought maybe this fish incident could be some kind of lesson. Maybe here he could educate. Imagine the nametag: *Edwin, Museum Educator.*

But when you in the black cape asked, "Why?" Ed again had no answer. Vader, you stood on a stool, looking down into the water, as if a bird's-eye view would help everything make sense. You were, maybe, four. You asked: "How he get in there?"

✳

What could Ed have taught you?

He could have taught you never to stand on a stool. But Ed was no teacher. Museum Educators were the ones with the knowledge, a pay grade above the Playworkers, and Ed knew he'd never last long enough to be promoted. He was the only employee without a college degree. The only one with a record. The only one old. What did Ed know? He was fifty-four. In prison, they'd let him lead a letter-writing class, which the museum's HR team had found promising. But, friends, you never wanted to write letters. You only ever wanted to do the things letters get written *about*—climbing, digging, laughing until your throat was sore, knocking, smashing, and pulling things down. And who could blame you? It wasn't your fault. It's just that Ed worried about his effectiveness, his abilities, his every step. The job was better than him and out to prove it. Though he was not hired under a probationary condition like his previous three jobs, he still felt under surveillance. He often acted a bit like a mannequin whose beard grew and limbs moved. Honestly, his bosses were sweet and smiling, but they always seemed to be too near—behind the curtain when he was with you on the Play Stage, in the walk-in freezer when he was pouring coffee, at the urinal when he was praying in the stall. Around every corner: a staff member. Not watching him, but just there. Ed was older than even the executive director, who on this day, the day of the fish, was away at a Play conference.

Or was she? Maybe she was in Tree Fort #4, watching Ed struggling to offer you answers. Friends, try again. Always: *Try again.*

Vader: "How the little fish get—"

"Some fish just eat other fish," Ed said. This was the job, playing and working and worrying alongside you friends. Naturally, the job also included picking up your dropped paintbrushes, sanitizing every Duplo that touched your mouth, and sometimes rescuing you from the rope tunnel as you wailed, shocked at how you ever ended up this far from the ground, Ed climbing up to scoop you, terrified of where to put his hands. No, the real job was telling you things from time to time. It may have looked easy, friends, but it could be hell. He knew what the uncareful words of adults could do. "And sometimes it's too much," Ed eventually added, about the eating. Outside, the band's song stopped. You just shook your plastic head.

Ed could never remember facts about the animals. Though you were bewildered by that tilapia swimming with two tailfins, your every inquiry was met with Ed's shrug or a handing off of the sticky note pad. If staff couldn't answer a question, you were to write questions on Post-its and press them to the Ag Lab desk. After close, Ed would research answers for: "Do snakes have pee pees?" "What frog name?" "Where does lightning?" Some of you were too young to write and simply scribbled. Your inkblots were questions he studied all the same.

"Have you ever seen anything like that?" the shift manager said. She was half Ed's age and amused. You were losing interest. Two of you wandered off. You with the glasses began leaping down the Ag Lab's short three-stair entrance. This area of the museum was raised a few feet above the main floor. It was a special place where, on that day, only one of you stayed—Vader.

The Wild Pond Life exhibit had stunk up the back of the museum for five weeks, and things died daily in different ways. Ed always tried to clear away any bodies before the doors opened. A catfish in the return hose. Two belly-up frogs with tadpoles pecking at their knees. Though the foot-long tiger salamander flourished, she creeped Ed out with her black stone eyes. Friends constantly asked if she was really alive.

Vader, you tapped at the glass tank and asked one final time: "Why?"

The shift manager shrugged: "Food chain."

Vader: "Food train?"

"More like food train *wreck*!" Ed said, too loud to be funny. You were silent. Everyone seemed to be wondering the same thing. The manager pointed to her heart. Ed didn't realize she was motioning for him to straighten his nametag.

"Anyway, what a teachable moment," she said, walking back to her desk hidden behind the Story Stage. Ed looked into the reflection of the glass, trying to fix his nametag. One day he'd worn it upside down for six hours.

From the window came the sour croon of a saxophone.

And then you, Vader, asked: "When you will save the Iowa darter?"

What Ed heard was the first time any friend had ever called the thin little fish by name, the title labeled on the wall placard—its proper, rightful name. Ed swelled with pride. "You're right," he said. "Iowa darter."

When Ed ran to the closet for a net, you clapped.

Ed's attitude toward the job was part pain in the ass, part unstoppable gratitude. Often in the last half hour of his shift, he cried secretly in the Kid's Quarry behind the big air filter because he'd been waiting for that moment all day, but also because: what a privilege. The sounds you made directing plays about bees, the greasy aroma of your birthday party pizzas, the look on your faces through the glass of the paint wall whenever two colors made a new one. There isn't a word for the feeling—happiness, guilt, gratitude, exhaustion, all mixed with a dash of fear that someone would realize very soon that they'd made a mistake hiring him.

The band outside moved to a new song, one with cymbals crashing. Ed held the net like a weapon, ready to plunge it into the water. For a second, he felt cavalier and confident. But then he paused, watching the tilapia swim along, noticing the way it moved as if bad things didn't happen, like this was just life. It was as if fish, too, made poor attempts to hide their crises. Ed began, for the first time, to feel bad for the tilapia. Maybe you did too. Maybe you saw that it'd simply messed up. And now it might die trying to swallow this mistake. But Ed also thought he saw in the thing's shifting eyes a willingness to die, like it'd be a necessary penance for all the other darters the tilapia had killed, ones who'd gone down much more easily.

You pumped your gloved fists and chanted: "Save him! Save him!"

And then Ed did it—shoved the net into the tank—and the sunfish, the guppies, and the bottom-feeders fled. You cheered. You would have your answer. You would learn whether the darter was still alive, or if it'd become part of its predator.

Vader, do you remember Ed chasing the tilapia with that tiny net? Throughout his young life, Ed had been afraid to swim in lakes, creeks, rivers, and even above ground pools because something scaly might brush his leg. He squirmed at fish, amphibians, insects, birds— any non-mammal felt like a monster. Once, a babysitter who knew little Eddy's fear of bees trapped some air in her hand and brought it toward him. Ed turned to run, but it was a wall. She laughed. She'd cornered him. She opened her hands and screamed—nothing was there. Her son had set fire to the school Ed would attend three years later. This was the only daycare his father could afford, and sometimes he wouldn't even pick Ed up, and the next morning he'd wake up on the dirty den floor of a strange house.

Then, in the war, it was not so much the men he killed, but the jungle beetles, dragonflies, mosquitoes fat with malaria.

Then, in the gravel parking lot of a Waverly, Iowa, bar—where a fight Ed didn't start ended in his opponent's pulpy face and barely twitching legs—it was a sharp-shelled snapping turtle, wide as a dinner plate, marching her babies out of the tallgrass.

And, at the museum, it was the way robins twitched after hitting the west wall window, how the museum's python, Scout, would lunge, wrap, and squeeze the already dead mice they fed him. The way bugs could get inside you. He preferred the Morning Move-N-Groove to the Monarch Larvae Harvest, the Paint Wall to the Lord Baltimore Barnyard.

And yet, friend, there he was swiping through the water, forearm submerged. He kept catching those slow, bloated goldfish by accident. The tilapia avoided capture easily, watching you through the glass, with its one eye saying, *You don't want to know.*

Ed needed a bigger net. You booed behind your dark plastic. The band outside repeated the same off-key measure of "Don't Stop Believin.'"

At first, you watched Ed rummage through the cabinet for another net, but then, you decided to act. You stood again on a stool, breaking museum rules. You reached over the water. The edge of the aquarium dug into your armpits. You dunked your black-gloved hand into the tank, and soon you held the tilapia above the water, still with its mouth full.

Ed turned and yelled a word we won't repeat, but it scared you. You dropped the fish onto the floor, the impact loud and wet.

The darter shot out the tilapia's mouth and slid beneath the small, wheeled desk the tank sat on. The bigger fish flopped, a beating heart on the floor.

But Ed went for the darter first. He unlatched the lock on the desk's wheels, moved the whole apparatus, and slid the victim fish out. He closed his hands around it like a secret bee.

"Open!" you demanded, and Ed unclasped one hairy hand.

From dorsal to tailfin—its back half—the darter looked fine. Its teal spine still glowed. But the front half was milky pink, maimed, with no eyes. It'd shriveled like cotton candy soaked.

The little fish was motionless. "We're too late," Ed said.

The tilapia, in a final act of defiance, stopped flopping on the floor. Ed told you to take the half darter as he gathered the tilapia into the net. You held your vinyl hands out like a cup. Ed transferred the mangled animal, no longer than a crayon, into them. Offering his trust to you, Ed let you be a friend, not just a visitor, but a helper, a human. Your breath was heavy, panting. You never removed the mask. There were no other friends around to see this moment. They were gone, over it. Off at lunch these friends asked their parents why, and why, and were never satisfied. Years later they'd ask a friend, a lover, a stranger in a bar what it felt like to be eaten.

Correction: half-eaten. Because the darter's tail still wagged. It gave one weak twitch in your hands, felt like a puppy licking your finger. Maybe you could hear its microscopic heartbeat. And you, friend, Vader—it was the moment you met something both a little dead and a little alive. This is exactly how we move through the world: half in, half out of the grave.

Your arms shook, holding the fish. Ed brought the tilapia just a touch into the water, and it slid out of the net, back into the tank

over which it held dominion. Then, Ed asked you for the darter.
You leaned down and whispered or kissed the little fish. Ed waited.

"We bury him?" you said. Ed just looked at you. For the first time
he thought hard about what kind of kid wears a black costume in
June. What kind of friend. He knew nothing about you. He never
asked questions. He even figured you for a boy. "Where we bury the
fish?" you said.

Ed had no clue. Ed imagined fish just lay down on the river floor
until bigger fish took all the pieces away. He held his hands out for the
body. You stood across from one another, both your hands cupped,
in the otherwise empty Agricultural Laboratory of the Mason-Dixon
Young Learners Museum. The metronome of the band across the street
finally silenced, one long trombone note whining through the air.

You gave Ed the fish. But he didn't know that the darter had any life
left. You did not tell him about its twitching in your palm. So, in his
hand, when that disfigured sliver gave another kick, Ed was shocked
and startled and dumped the half-dead thing back into the water.

"No!" you screamed.

And here Ed turned the tables on you. He asked, "Why?"

It was all he ever wanted to ask.

And you had no answer, only an urgent sense of injustice, an
innate certainty that something here was not fair or normal. And
when you saw through the glass that the tilapia had already scooped
the darter back into its mouth, you acted. Vader, you jumped toward
the aquarium, grabbed its edge with both gloves—and you pulled,
and the narrow desk below the tank began to roll, and Ed backed out
of the way like this was normal, natural, the ordered world at work,
and you kept pulling until the wheels reached the first low step, and
down it went like a tower of blocks, and crushed you.

✳

The warm water was the first thing you felt, the musk of algae the first thing you smelled. The first thing you saw: sunfish bouncing in puddles of black water, in tangles of your long blond hair. The tank's shatter was the last thing you heard. You were unconscious before you ever saw the blood, or felt the shards, or heard Ed's hoarse voice explode with questions.

Every day that week, families would arrive at the front door of the Mason-Dixon Young Learner's Museum to find it locked. Friends asked moms why. How? What do you mean *closed*? They didn't even care for answers. All they wanted was in, banging fists against the glass doors.

Ed didn't have to be asked to leave the museum. He lay in bed for days with his nametag on and straight. He's out west now, a sooth-sayer on some low stage. He tries to explain the ways in which the course of your young life can veer.

You lived but lost a lot of blood, Vader, a lot of memory. In fact, to this day, when you think of that museum, you remember some-thing else entirely. You remember a loud, driving song, a lot of sun, the sound of cymbals washing out. You remember a worried man kneeling in the sod of the Lord Baltimore Barnyard, digging a fish a grave with his hands.

HICCUPS FOREVER

An hour after it happened, I watched our house explode. Friday, in History 9. Evan's phone got passed around under the tables. I was the last to watch, dropped his phone, cracked the screen. Then the hiccups came. They haven't left. You can still watch the video on YouTube. It's there. Search "York County Home Disintegrates in Gas Explosion." A cop car parked on our block had a dashcam going. It's a normal day. Spring. Blue sky. Mr. Simms has Groucho on a walk. On the left, a white house goes pufferfish. For a millisecond it's still our house, just expanded, with space in between every piece. You can see sky through each tiny seam. My green room spreads out. Then: confetti. Black confetti. Our dog dies. Groucho barks. Mr. Simms runs past the camera. Nobody knew it was my house when they handed me the phone. They don't even know my name is Cara. I watched it anyway. I've watched it a lot. The video played on Facebook all weekend. People said it was awesome, which was weird. But I shared it too. Twenty-seven likes—a personal record. La Quinta's manager put my parents in separate rooms. The other guests couldn't sleep with all their loud-ass blame. My sister Jenna told me, "Kiss everything normal bye," and "I can't sleep with you making those noises." So I've been lying on a booth in the hotel breakfast nook every night, wondering what she means and hiccupping. Nobody's sharing the video anymore, but I still watch it. A lot. On the computer in the lobby. Full-screened, reversed, dragging the button left across the page. Slow as possible. It's cool. Every piece has somewhere to go. Everything shrinks back together. My hiccups stop. It's weird. Played forward, the house pieces float there until they disappear. That's the future, I think. What Jenna means. When I let go of the mouse, I hiccup. Eight seconds: our house is over. Even the smoke's gone. Just blue. Springtime. Groucho barking. Like we were never there. But watching in reverse, it's different. In reverse, I can breathe. Plus it's prettier, like a party when everyone finally shows up, before anybody starts to leave.

BREAKTHROUGH MAILBOXES OF SOUTHERN PENNSYLVANIA

Across the street, the young, blond entrepreneurs have opened for business at the end of their driveway, cardboard signs advertising the sale of their small sister. She sits in the gravel, wearing a leash. Her hair's in pigtails. Her brothers are screaming. No cars stop, though many swerve as they pass the property, nearly mowing over *Fallingwater*, Rhonda's masterpiece mailbox.

Rhonda watches through the French window of her rancher, stress-squeezing a bottle of tacky glue, a tiny sconce on her newest model drying crooked. It's the final day of her bereavement leave, but her mind is on last month's accident—when a rubbernecking motorcyclist wiped out and totaled her *Monticello* mailbox, its miniature Corinthian pillars catching in his silver beard. Her art, erased. That day, the kids were playing a game called Semper Fi! where they pile inside the recycling tote, wait for the hum of a coming vehicle, and pop out jack-in-the-box style, screaming military slogans in hopes of goosing the driver.

Theirs is a bent, busy street on the edge of York City, Pennsylvania, where motorists, having endured a slew of long red lights, like to pretend the new 35 MPH signs say 53. Rhonda's property starts where the sidewalk dissolves into a gravelly shoulder and Tower Avenue doglegs out of town. In the apex of the bend stands her mailbox—clearly visible but totally vulnerable.

Today the two boys, maybe nine and six, shout at every vehicle that passes the property. "One hundred percent organic girl! Listen up, shitheads! Only one in stock!" If a car goes by without reaction—not even a honk or a jostle—it's the middle finger for its rearview mirror. The boys have stubby, ugly middle fingers, like chopped-up hot dogs. She's never met their father but imagines his hands are rough, dirt in the creases, grease in the lifeline.

Closing the curtain, Rhonda shakes her head and decides to intervene. She enters her garage, hoping to sneak up on the kids from the side and convey to them the danger—is it too rash to call it terror?—they're bringing to this neighborhood, to their own troubled family, to her art.

With the garage light off, she bumps into the *Chrysler Building*, stubs a toe on the stairs of *The Met*. She loves to walk through this room full of mailboxes pretending it's a dark gallery the tourists can never find. *And this piece,* she hears the docent whisper, *was the first, started the month of the artist's divorce. This one's named after her son who never calls.* The voice fades as she descends the driveway.

"In fact, we'll pay *you* to take her!" the boys yell as she limps past her hedgerow and across the street. "Fire sale! Fire sale!"

"Boys," she says, as if they're her kids and not strangers who moved in a few months ago, "you'll regret the day someone stops and, you know, suddenly she's gone."

"She who?" says, maybe, Derek. Derek is the name she hears their father yell most often.

"Your dear sister," Rhonda says.

"All she ever does is sing," he says, taking the end of the leash and whipping it around his head like a lasso. A passing Subaru swerves at the road's bend—missing *Fallingwater*—then speeds off.

In the silence left behind, Rhonda hears it, the girl whisper-singing a wordless song.

"I think it's pleasant," Rhonda says, though the noise grates. "Like a bird."

"We don't want a bird," the other boy says, fists in his swim trunks. "We want waffles!"

"Isn't today a school day?" Rhonda asks. It's late September.

"Belgian waffles, lady."

"So you want to give your sister away for waffles, but I wonder—what would your mother think?"

"Do you see her?" says Derek. "Do you see our mom, like, around?"

Rhonda kneels in the stones to make eye contact with the girl, who can't yet be four years old, whose mouth opens a bit wider to sing, "Our mother's in the clicker."

"The clicker?" Rhonda asks, squinting at the girl. "Is this some kind of riddle?"

"Shit, the TV clicker," says Derek, pointing with an invisible remote, pressing his thumb, hating this channel, the Judgment Channel, this obnoxious episode featuring a sixty-seven-year-old, gray-hair-hanging-to-her-ass, nosy "artist" named Rhonda. The other boy comes over and tucks the ends of her long, gray hair into Rhonda's back khaki pocket. All the children laugh.

A weathered Buick approaches slowly, the engine popping, the window sliding down.

"Go get jobs!" comes a young, hard shout. When Rhonda turns, the car speeds away, the back tires spraying stones, but it swerves—the joke so funny that the driver's lost his grip—and there they go, off the road. *Fallingwater* falls.

The teen reverses, gets out, pulls a black knit hat off his head, and asks if what he hit belongs to her. The kids run inside, Derek pulling his sister along with the leash. "Swear to God, lady," the driver says. "I'll replace this, uh—was that a mailbox?" Rhonda picks up one of the house's tan cantilevers. The blue cellophane creek blows through the neighbor's yard.

"Listen—I *have* a job." She points the piece at him. "And I have to go back tomorrow."

That night, because it's warm and she is able, fit, focused on longevity, Rhonda walks five blocks to the YorkArts Center and drops off her *Hemingway House* for their yearly local juried show. Last fall, her *Monticello* was chosen (so was nearly every other submission), but it was displayed sloppily on a low stool behind the snack table. Alone, she had left the reception early.The clerk who takes her piece smiles as an ornamental six-toed cat falls from the house's balcony. She tries to explain *Fallingwater* to him. Truly, it had been her landmark work. Often Rhonda worries that she's not really an artist, only kind of clever and a little annoying. An image comes into her mind as she walks home—her mailboxes going two for ten at a quick and careless estate sale auction. "Two for five!" her son yells to the bored buyers. "Fuck it—free! Fire sale!"

On the way, she stops at Turkey Hill and buys a giant Pepsi slushie. She sucks it down in the parking lot until her brain freezes. She's had three weeks off to mourn Alan's death. Not that she needed any time at all to grieve her ex-husband—they'd been divorced eight years and she hadn't loved him since—when? College? Back when she was painting and he still watched her like a television? She was entitled to the benefit, though, and since her boss is a creep, she milked it. Her plan was to turn the leave into a self-funded artist residency, an opportunity to abandon her current mode of imitation and finally design something original—a home nobody had ever seen.

However, apart from finishing *Fallingwater*, she'd wasted the time watching and worrying about the kids across the street. She wondered what care looked like to other people, wondered when neglect became abuse. They weren't really the same, were they? Alan had hit their son, AJ, five times during his eighteen years in the house, and Rhonda remembers each one—especially the first, how she just stood at the sink, scrubbing so hard the steel wool ate a hole through the tin baking sheet.

The WALK sign is on, but she's not walking.

For eighteen years, Rhonda taught crafting classes and shelved books at the library, but after Alan left, she had to find a job with health insurance. For a while she worked as a cafeteria aide in the high school, then three years ago she took a job at a counseling practice called Total Hope Life Services. When she applied, she imagined working with at-risk youth and young mothers, guiding them past the failures of their parents, maybe using arts-and-crafts therapy. But instead, she checks patients in at the front desk and suffers the requests of the staff's four "Hope Therapists" and Troy, her needy boss. He's the owner, and he believes in hugs. To work he rides a bicycle that—after fifteen minutes of Troy grunting and sweating in the lobby—folds up to the size of a briefcase. Everything he wears is wicking. "*Wick*ing," he explains to Rhonda weekly. "Feel it. Rub. The sweat comes out of me, but then this stuff just—*fwwwp*—wicks it right off." He smells like her son's old hockey bags in the back of the garage. Every morning, Troy's shoes click loudly down the hallway, disturbing the appointments, leaving tough, dark marks.

Today, when Rhonda returns to the office, it's worse than she remembered. Troy has hung new "art" on the walls, one print still bearing a half-torn Target price sticker. There's a four-panel image of a daisy carrying through each season, a montage of mantras, a gray-scale Eiffel Tower.

Rhonda sits at her desk, hidden by stacks of counseling notes to be filed, when Troy clomps into the waiting room.

"Rhon!" he says, folding in a handlebar. "Did you have a great bereavement?"

"Well," she says. "I mean—I think it was healthy."

"You look like a wrung sponge," he says, eyes on his shoes. On her first day, Rhonda was forced to take a "technology test" during which Troy stood behind her, watching as she navigated the practice's webpage, reports portal, and billing system. Rhonda types with two fingers. She knows it's abnormal, but she's actually quite fast. "Oh no," Troy had said, dropping his hands to her shoulders. "I see you're a pecker." When he said it, she'd been concentrating too hard to feel insulted, but she felt it later, and cried quietly into her sangria glass at Applebee's.

Now he's at the side of the desk, leaning over the folders, spotting them with sweat.

"How are you, Troy?" she says.

"Buried, Rhon. Just swamped. Not easy working two jobs while you're off. Really, I've broken many a sweat this last month."

"Good thing you've got your wicking."

"Do I sense an attitude today?"

"No, no. Sorry." She rises, takes refuge near the printer.

"Rhonda." He's behind her now. "You know I'm sorry for your loss, right?"

"Thanks," she says, turning and accidentally stepping into his hug.

Surprising herself, she leans against him, lets out a loud breath. Her eyes close for a long, unpleasant moment.

"Do me a favor. Stop by my office at lunch. We should debrief about the bereavement."

"We should?" she says, thinking of the neighbor kids—what are they doing for lunch?

"Policy," he says. "A few questions, you know. *T*'s to cross, lowercase *j*'s to dot."

"It sounds like a grief pop quiz."

"Okay," he says, nodding. "So it is an attitude."

There's a flimsy, rusted, head-high filing cabinet in the break room where the Office Communal Foods forms are kept, charts on which the employees are supposed to record the amount of shared items they've consumed each day, like coffee, sugar, ketchup, and, for some reason, ice cubes. This morning, Rhonda's alone with the cabinet, fighting with the top drawer. The massive case tilts forward easily, especially when the top drawer's pulled all the way out. Others have complained about this in the past, complaints Troy has waved away as part of his employees' secret plan to bankrupt the company with needless overhead expenses.

Pulling the top drawer farther out, Rhonda imagines what another month off could do for her art. She opens a second drawer. What will Troy ask in this meeting? She opens a third drawer, and the metal tower lurches forward, and she screams before she feels a thing.

The next day, the kids across the street have a new, disturbing scheme running. They've stuck their sister in the crotch of an oak alongside the road. From the perspective of passing cars, you can't even tell she's up there. In the driveway, about ten yards off, the boys go down on one knee and level cap rifles at the orange leaves. Every time a car guns around the bend, one of the brothers yells, "Open fire!" and they shoot, their bodies rocking with dramatic kickback. The girl then sidles out of the tree and falls four feet to the ground, where she lies splayed, tongue out and eyes rolled back. She's not a bad actress, Rhonda notes. But it's wrong. It just is.

They're boosting her back into the tree when Rhonda rolls up on her knee scooter. *Fallingwater* has been replaced by a model of the New York Guggenheim she's not especially proud of, its spiraled white atrium resembling a sort of toilet tank.

"Are you two trying to destroy my mailboxes?" she says from the shoulder. Startled, the boys turn. The girl slips from the branch, crumples to the ground.

"Illuminati confirmed!" they shout.

Rhonda doesn't understand, but wants to.

"One," Derek says, "you're always watching us."

"Two," the other boy says, "you want to control our every move."

"Three," Derek says, "you look like a witch, you make shitty weird castles, and . . ."

"Seven," the girl sings, "you get no mail!"

"Illuminati confirmed," the younger boy says, nodding. The insults, silly as they are, still sting. Rhonda looks at the slate-gray prefab house behind them, its Veneerstone siding and hollow Corinthian pillars. Yeah, the place is big, but she can tell it's empty inside.

"You know, I lost someone, too," she says. "My husband. Plus, my son never visits."

"Oh, no," says the younger boy, "the video!" He runs to a lawn chair and grabs a handheld camera.

"I'm your neighbor," she says, looking at Derek. "And neighbors can talk to each other."

"Wyatt—give me that!" says Derek, pressing buttons on the camera. "We're making a YouTube. If enough people watch it, you get money, and then maybe a TV show."

"Or concert!" says the girl. Her shirt reads I CUT MY OWN HAIR. "Concert, too, right Wyatt?"

"Yes, Jessie. God," Wyatt says.

"The best part," says Derek, "is editing it on the computer. Like, when people drive by, you can zoom in on their faces. You can put them on a loop."

"Yeah," says Wyatt. "They look like this." He lifts his eyebrows and crosses his eyes.

"Yeah," says Derek, "it's like—" He does a droopy zombie face.

"Like—" Jessie says, mussing her hair and shoving out her tongue.

"Like this?" Rhonda says, screwing up her face like Troy folding his bicycle.

The children scream with laughter. Wyatt grabs her hand and whispers, "Wanna come inside and see?"

Her suspicion about their home is correct—there's nothing inside. The walls are off-white and endless. The vinyl flooring mimics granite. There is practically no natural light. She doesn't see any clear signs of abuse, unless you consider the air-conditioning that blasts from the vents to be a form of punishment.

"It's like a cave in here," she says. "I'm freezing." But Wyatt assures her that Illuminati witches can't freeze. Rhonda looks at her phone and sees an email from Troy with the subject heading "RE: Workers' Comp." ("Just some *t*'s to cross here, but I'm curious . . .") She puts the phone away. Jessie grabs her by the ring finger and pulls her to the living room, where Rhonda's scooter catches on the lip of the carpet. A Hannah Montana poster is spread on the floor, held down by an array of action figures.

"This is my boy band," Jessie says. "They sing on YouTube."

The living room is just a pleather sectional, a giant television, and three windows with the blinds drawn. Rhonda used to own a TV but mostly kept it in the closet. A quiet man, a reader, Alan hauled it out only for special occasions, like the Super Bowl or a Vietnam documentary. They'd always seen TV as a bad socializer, like video games. Her own mother spent years in front of a TV, bound to her recliner, Rhonda only a bother. Because she was alone, Rhonda didn't blame her as much as she blamed entertainment, its usurping power to distract.

Jessie turns the TV to VH1 and begins to sing, though no one on the show is singing. It's a reality show apparently focused on poolside fistfights, but the girl hears a tune in it. Screens don't seem to be stifling these kids' creativity, though maybe they've made them fame-obsessed. But doesn't everyone dream of being seen? Rhonda often fantasizes about seeing her work in a museum, of giving a great, brief speech to a sharp crowd of admirers. "Have a ball," she'd say. "Drink the wine! Oh, and try the mini-quiches!" She'd wear a loud dress, something geometric and yellow, her hair done up and remarkable.

"Dad says I can't be famous. Derek says Dad's a bully. Miss F. says no bullies in Bible school."

"Wait," Rhonda says. "When will your father be home? When does he get off work?"

Though the three voices come from different rooms, they all ring out together in the same practiced monotone: "However long it takes, for fuck's sake!" Jessie holds out the last syllable on *sake*, pitching it up an octave. The voices echo through the empty house. Rhonda thinks of what she'd do with a place like this. Ever since she and Alan closed on the rancher, she had anticipated a bigger home, something more ornate, a structure she could work with, a house that might inspire her to pick up a brush again. It'd been a big upgrade from her mother's single-wide, but she'd always thought it was a first step to something better.

The first time Alan hit their son, AJ was four. Alan was on the phone and AJ was beneath the breakfast table, calling his father's name. When he pulled the placemat from the end of the table, bringing his father's breakfast shattering to the floor, he scrambled out to find Alan's arm flying back against his face.

"All he wanted was your attention!" Rhonda yelled at Alan afterwards.

"I reacted," Alan said, the line still live, the phone hugging his red face. "I just reacted!"

He would react again when AJ was nine. And again when he was eleven. Fifteen. Eighteen. And Rhonda, each time, would react, too—react by wondering how she could love a man whose instincts she couldn't trust. She tried. She couldn't. It didn't work. Why did she wait for *him* to leave? This is the question that her art can't formulate, that her son can't ask, that these poor neighbors could never answer.

"And his name Momma," Jessie says, holding up a shirtless, wounded GI Joe, and Rhonda sees the lip of a bruise on the girl's upper arm. She reaches out and pulls Jessie's sleeve further back.

The girl jerks away. "Hey!"

Suddenly Rhonda feels warm, nervous, like an intruder. For all anyone here knows, she's a threat to this family. Following them inside was a dumb idea. She wheels out into the foyer, past what she notices now is a giant ragged hole in the drywall. She doesn't ask.

"Where go?" Jessie says. Derek and Wyatt come sliding down the hall in socks.

"What the hell? I was gonna show you the video," Derek says. "It's just loading."

"And I made you this," Wyatt says, holding out a sandwich on a plate. Rhonda takes it from him, smiles, flips up the hearty bread. Ham, Brie. Is that apple?

"Pear," Wyatt says, smiling. Jessie rushes out into the foyer and hands her the clicker. Rhonda takes the hefty remote, feels its gummy buttons.

"Dad told us he put her ashes in there," Derek says. "So we can't ever lose it."

Rhonda tries to change the channel, but it doesn't reach. The credits keep rolling over two lovers crying in a cabana. "My ex-husband's wife, Theresa," she says, "had his ashes made into a little silver gemstone. She wears him on a ring."

"That's disgusting," Derek says, and his siblings nod. It really is.

Wyatt grabs the remote from Rhonda, shakes it near his ear. "Duh. There's nothing in here."

"Dad's a liar," Derek says, and his siblings fall silent.

Rhonda's halfway down the driveway when their father's truck whips in, nearly clipping her cast. From the doorway, the kids are calling: "Don't leave! You're not a witch!" Rhonda scoots through the grass, toward the safety of the road and, just beyond it, her own house.

Behind her, the truck door slams. "Excuse me," the man says. She's only ever seen him getting in and out of the truck—never in the yard with the kids, never on the porch, never taking walks or in the driveway working on projects. "Do you have business here?"

She keeps rolling until she reaches the road, a demilitarized zone. "Lady?" he says, his voice close at her back.

"The kids," she says, angling around toward him. "They, uh . . . well."

"Kids? My kids? Those kids in there who just lost their mother?"

"I know, I know, but—" she says, backing toward the road.

"Oh, you know? You're a know-it-all. Well, do you know where your property ends?"

"Listen, they broke my mailbox. Their reckless games. It's happened twice now."

"That one there?" he says, leaning to see past her. Rhonda stares at his suit, his leather shoes—brown and shining, but scuffed. She inches farther away from him, closer to home. He laughs. "I'm not sure they couldn't have done any more damage than you done."

A passing car honks at Rhonda, whose cast juts out into the demented road. "Get out of the fucking way!" the driver shouts from the window.

"What happened to your leg there?" the man says to Rhonda's back. She's pushing out across Tower Avenue. "Don't suppose my kids are to blame for that, too?"

Rhonda arrives home shaking. She wants only one thing: to work. To make art. But she can't work in the living room—not with that house across the street, the lights flashing on and off, the doors slamming. And it's too cold in the cramped kitchen. And the back porch is swamped with ladybugs. She hates this fucking house, always has. In AJ's old room, she spreads her materials on the bed and begins a strange new . . . what? It's not clear. She wings it. She paints the crooked siding a dark stone. Nearly black. Bars in the windows. No windows at all.

Even with Joni Mitchell's *Blue* at full volume, Rhonda can hear the father screaming. There have been sharp, lone shouts before, but this seems to be a full performance. She grabs her phone to call the police—maybe just a noise complaint—then hesitates. An old thought comes to her, one she's hated for decades: Who is *she* to claim to know the proper way for a father to act? Is it better to live with a mean man or none at all? If she steps in, things could get worse. The kids could be taken away. She stares at the phone. There's a beautiful alert for a missed call from AJ, which she immediately returns.

Her son is worried about her injury, the fact that she hasn't been working for over a month. When he coughs out the words *group home*, Rhonda interjects that she is sixty-two—though she's really sixty-four—and those places are for eighty-year-olds. AJ asks, "Why are you crying?" and she hangs up.

He calls back.

"Talk to me," he says.

"How? You never call."

"I'm calling now. I just called."

Rhonda feels a sick sinking in her gut, like a car cresting a country hill. "We need to talk about your father."

"You want to talk about why you didn't go to his funeral?"

"He abused you, AJ. Don't you see that?"

"Are you serious? I was there, Mom. I had to hide my own bruises. I saw it again and again. I still see it." He's trying hard not to shout, and she loves him for it. "But I forgave him. We reconciled."

"When?"

"Years ago, when he moved to New Mexico."

"When he left me."

"Yes, we talked about it for hours. It was awful. But I had to find a way to forgive him."

"What about me?"

"You?"

"Have you forgiven me?"

"For what?"

The line holds quiet.

"For the neglect?" AJ says.

"The *neglect*?" Rhonda says. She needs water. "What are you saying? I meant—I mean, because I never stopped him. Somehow I just hid. I ignored it."

"Mom, if you don't see how *that* is neglect, then how can I forgive you?"

Saturdays, Rhonda always switches her mailbox, but today she sleeps late. The argument with AJ knocked her down like five NyQuil, and now she can't remember where it ended. She's heavy in the bed, an anchor out of water. Turning over, she sees the dark, unfinished monstrosity she'd been making the night before and, beside it, her phone, which she checks: only a voicemail from Troy, about workers' comp, and he misses her, and there's a meeting with a lawyer.

At noon, she pushes out to switch her mailbox. This week is *Glass House*, after the famous home of Philip Johnson—a simpler piece, but she's always fantasized a life with nothing to hide. The sky looks ready for rain. The neighbor's truck is home. At the end of their driveway, the boys are tied to their own green plastic mailbox. A sign reads: FREE, O.B.O.

"It's a new game!" Wyatt yells to her. "It's called See How You Like It."

"Noooo," Derek corrects him. "Dad says it's Taste Your Own Medicine."

Rhonda turns around slowly, kicks her way back to the garage.

"Wait, wait!" Derek calls. "Dad doesn't get the filming part. He's not even recording! There won't be anything to put on YouTube. Go get us a camera, Rhonda."

"Or, wait," Wyatt says. "Just take us!"

"Yeah, Rhonda," Derek says. "We're free!"

The handheld camcorder was her gift to AJ one Christmas. She watches the little screen while she wheels through the house. She'd hoped he would make home videos, but the memory card is full of bootlegged movies from his friends' houses. *Air Bud* recorded on a camcorder so AJ could watch it in his room, beneath the covers, alone.

She's deleting, clearing space, hitting the trash can button again and again, when her cell phone rings. Her instinct is to ignore it. Could it be the final call from Troy, the one that says she's being fired?

No, it's from YorkArts. They've passed on her piece, and would she come pick it up at her earliest convenience? She drops the phone and leaves it on the floor. She will not cry. In the garage, she rolls right over the steps of *The Met*. It makes such a satisfying crunch.

Outside, she sets the camera on top of *Glass House* and frames the neighbors. Wait until the police see this. "Ready?" she says and clicks the red button. The boys begin to act like victims, straining against their ropes, grasping at the thin air.

"The Illuminati is pulling the strings!" they yell. Their voices fade behind her as she pushes off toward the city. "Mom! Mommy, help us!"

Rhonda powers up the sidewalk, head down, toward the city. She's got video proof of abuse, but the policemen at the desk don't want to watch her video. She shoves it in front of them. "Clever," they say, ignoring her other evidence—bruises on the kids, holes in the wall, how often they seem to be absent from school. The officers scratch a few notes, but neither asks for names or an address. "You ever heard of a free country?" one mumbles.

From the police station Rhonda goes to the gallery. "Thank you," says the clerk who hands over her mailbox. Without tears, she thanks him back, though what for? Outside, she has to work to balance the piece on the handlebars of her knee scooter, and just as she's ready to push off, the door to the building swings open. Out comes a man whose feet click against the sidewalk. A canvas the size of a sports-bar television obscures his head—a crude, cartoonish-looking pair of legs, the left one snapped in half and bleeding. The man puts down the painting, unlocks his bicycle from the no-parking sign. His legs and arms are slick with wicking. A sweat coats her boss's face. "Troy," she says as he tries to mount his bike with the awkward, violent painting under his arm. "Wait!" she says. "I didn't know you were a painter."

"Well, Rhon. I guess I'm not," he says. "Not according to these people."

"What is this?" she says, pointing to the canvas.

"My accident." The sweat on his face might be tears as he explains how a surgeon had to remove a whole section of shattered bone. A car ran him off the road. His left leg's a quarter-inch shorter now. "The bike shoes help a lot, kind of even out my step."

It's quiet. No cars pass. "I'm sorry that happened to you." Rhonda takes a breath and adds, "Don't touch me at work anymore."

"You mean hugging?"

"Actually, I mean," she says, "I quit."

Troy sighs, mounts his bike with the canvas squeezed under his armpit, and gives no wave. Rhonda's nearly home before the mailbox slips from her handlebars and tumbles to the street. Perhaps a passing bus will smash it. She doesn't wait around to see.

When Rhonda finally wheels up to her house, she feels very light. It's possible her broken foot has disappeared—that's how little she's aware of it. Unless she looks down at her body beneath her head, she can't guarantee any of it is there. This feels different. Not good, not bad, just empty.

The boys are still tied to the mailbox. Derek's shirt is pulled up to his nose and he's crying into the collar. Wyatt, sprawled and kicking the air, looks like fresh roadkill. The sun, on its arc back down, heads for the top of their house. Hours they've been out here.

"It's over now," Rhonda says, reaching down for the knot of plastic rope. "Game over."

"Did we win?" Wyatt asks. Rhonda nods, though she's not convinced. The knot's so small, and impossibly tight. She tries, using her teeth, then gives up. As it falls from her hands, she reaches down again, her leg slipping off the scooter, and she tips onto the lawn. Here she lies, watching the sky turn pink. Ladybugs hover on flat paths through the air. The boys lean back in the dirt beside her. The rope around their waists has rubbed the skin of their hips raw. This is something she can see with her eyes. Evidence. What else? She sees that she will not be able to save them. And a glass mailbox, across the street, throwing around the last light of the sun, delivering what only a fool would view as hope.

"I am going to go home. I am going to go home and call the police until they come."

"Why are you talking like that?" Wyatt says.

Rhonda struggles to her feet and back onto her scooter.

"Why are you leaving?" Derek says. "Can we come?"

The boys' protests grow louder as she crosses Tower Avenue a final time. There are quick cars coming, but they're still far away. Behind her, the boys strain at the ends of their leashes, trying to chase. They pull and pull and stretch the rope, and when the post gives way, they fall forward into the road's stony shoulder, shocking an approaching driver, who swerves. The car crashes through *Glass House* and hurtles over the hedgerow. Unable to stop, it levels her.

The day before her U-Haul comes, Rhonda hosts a garage sale that AJ calls a gallery opening. A few dozen people wander by and walk inside. There's the *Robie House*, *Chrysler*, and the *Capitol*. There's *Farnsworth*, *Taliesin*, *Hollyhock*, *Eames*. Look at the dented *Met*, the *Unity Temple*. Visitors stroll the space as Rhonda watches from a wheelchair, woozy on pain pills but bursting with nerves. The strangers touch; she does not stop them. No prices are posted, but if they ask, she says, "Make an offer." She doesn't count the money. Each sale, she takes another pill, dry.

By early evening she's hardly awake. The sun falls low enough to shine directly into the garage—a tunnel of light she feels her chair creeping toward.

AJ puts his arm around her shoulder. "Theresa's here to see you," he says.

Rhonda opens her eyes and sees a dark-haired, middle-aged woman who takes her hand and shakes it.

"Alan told me you were an artist," she says. "Undiscovered." The ring on her finger is charcoal-colored, but glowing. Could that be him? "Oh, here," she says. "You can hold it."

Rhonda shakes her head. Theresa hugs AJ, walks the gallery, opens her wallet. When she leaves, it's with the *Unity Temple* under her arm, heels clicking on the driveway.

"Do me a favor?" Rhonda asks AJ, but hears no answer. "Can you make sure the kids across the street are okay? I'm sorry, honey. But can you do that for them?"

Soon the garage door is sliding down, but Jessie sneaks beneath it, singing. She's wearing a bathing suit, waving to Rhonda, skipping down the rows and peering into windows, peeling open little doors as if picking a lash from an eye. She finds an unfinished mailbox tucked back in the corner—a pitch-black house with pillars, a porch that looks foreign yet familiar—and gathers it into her arms. Her song gets loud, louder, thundering as she approaches, trying to wake the artist from her sleep.

"Why's this one empty?" the girl says, setting the house on the card table.

Rhonda leans forward. She wants to answer, so she peers inside, watching, as if something might emerge.

"They all are," Rhonda says. And together they reach to fix the little garage door, which is either falling closed or coming open.

COUNTY MAP (DETAIL)

Town's got ten churches, no library. More cop cars than stores. Four laundries. Not counting the ones inside the Best Westerns. Yes, there's a second Best Western. Everyone has an opinion on which is Better. The West Best Western is the Better Best Western, goes an old incantation. Here, a hole opens up in the ground if you stumble. We have guns. We have running, but never for fun. Of course we have running water, what do you think this is, Not America? Who told you that? But I never said it was potable, now spit. We even have a water tower, though it was, as a prank, painted black. The monument outside the burned library shows an old man (our town's founder) holding a snake (by the name of Lonely) and it too is painted that. Not a prank, if you ask the artist. Which our part-time and only reporter did. And soon after the interview aired, the East Best Western's Ballroom B became home to an unruly congregation of equal parts pranksters and artists, gathered finally to draw boldly the line between them. Bedlam. Shouting like quicksand. No mediators. No counselors. One therapist with a waitlist. Did I mention our thirteen mediums? All homes are warmed by oil stored in basement tubs, a bobber that drops to warn the owner there's nothing left to burn but rust. At three a.m., I've got twenty dollars for anyone who can tell apart an artist from a hoaxer as they stagger along Locust Ave. Dryer lint's what gallops down Main Street like tumbleweed. Excuse my failure to fill in the gaps. Twenty-three, no, twenty-four

lots gone to seed. Are you sold yet? We've got no gold. We've got a
Cash-for-Gold. Had two, in fact, until the second was reborn as a
credit union. Verizon store morphed back into a Kwik Trip. What
else what else what else what else? My brain's turning both its pockets
out. I'm on empty. Don't laugh. Town's got . . . had . . . Our addresses,
yes—they all end in halves. You hope it's plenty.

WATCHPERSON

On Sunday, May 29th at 5:26 p.m. the Deliver Area Police responded to an auto theft incident on Turtlebell Road. The victims were a thirty-two-year-old couple driving east for a Memorial Day party. Ash gray Honda Civic, 1999. Spinach casserole in the backseat. The victims advised they were surprised to see a lone flagger stationed at the bend by Baylor Rock. No signs or cones warned of the flagger, the victims reported, he was just there. The victims reported they did slow as the flagger's sign was spun to stop. The victims reported they did idle. Did wait. Did wonder what the fuss was. The victims described the suspect as looming and beanpole and sunburnt to the point of blister and he did stare at them blankly for what the female said was one minute but the male said was six. The victims did conference about the length of time the looming flagger stared, and I noticed two springs of black hair had strayed from her updo, and editorially bounced at her neckline like home-phone cords. As the reporting officer, I will do my best to restrict opinion and avoid lies, though I left one in the first sentence. The victims landed on 90 seconds. The suspect did turn his fist in the air, motioning for the female victim to drop her driver's-side window. (She advised that, on trips to his parent's place, she always drove, as he did need to perform various breathing exercises, his parents being quite intense, disapproving, well-off, and loud. Victim used the word looming again. She said, for example, my hair, and pointed to her updo. Before each family party she sees a hairdresser. So she won't be pitied. She smiled through her make-up. Editorial: I felt as if the male victim resented the female victim's release of these details, seeing as how he pulled his shirt up to his forehead, blond hair spilling from the collar). After 90 seconds, the beanpole flagger, the suspect, he did in fact move toward the car with his sign in hand, still turned to STOP. The victim did roll her window down halfway, but reluctantly. As the flagger leaned down into the open window, he dropped his sign to the ground and said, "Happy Memorial Day. Sorry for the hassle, but I'm going to need you both to step out of the car." The victim advised she did not ask the suspect why and responded by cranking her window back up with gusto. The man was crazy, the victim advised, dangerous. Editorial: I believed her. I still do. She said his eyes were like a cream soup in which two red beans floated, half-submerged.

The victim did put the car in drive, did surge forward. The suspect was jostled. Not knocked or struck or attacked, the victims agreed, but jostled. She sped ahead, snapping in half the suspect's sign, until she reached the bend and saw a line of orange cones. For a second she doubted her instincts and felt that the stop was maybe, somehow, in fact, normal, and legal, and that driving around the hairpin turn of Baylor Rock would be unsafe, like what if it was a gas tanker back there, burning, so she pumped the brakes again. She closed her eyes. Her boyfriend did pull his shirt up to his nose, covering his mouth (this must be some kind of compulsion). The victim advised she did glance into her rearview mirror but saw no one, and she wondered if the suspect had fled, or if indeed they'd hurt him, was he okay?—

—a knife blade punched her window. And again. Little divots in the glass. Matte black survival knife. Flying into the pane like a bird, beak-first. Editorially speaking. Both victims advised that the flagger, knife long as a hand, did stab at the window repeatedly. Total of six times. Lost in shock, the victim admitted she could not move the car forward or backward, her feet and hands feeling stuck in blocks of ice, and the flagger ripped open the back door, reached in and gripped the victim by her hair. She said he smelled like gasoline. Is that a clue? I recorded it all. Everything the victims reported. It's here in my notes. I was doing my best.

The suspect again demanded they exit the car, and this time the victims did exit. The suspect demanded and then received their cell phones, which he placed beneath the front tire. He then commandeered the driver's seat and, idling, did reach into the backseat for the casserole. The victims reported he took one large bite of the dish, shoveling the food to his mouth with the knife. The male victim, I'm guessing he did nothing, except maybe breathe. The suspect then spit the bite out the window, more or less at her. He did peel away and crush their phones. The weather was warm, but not yet humid. The sun (metaphorical) was like a conscience. The suspect took the bend at Baylor Rock slow, brake lights flaring—suddenly, it seemed, afraid of the construction he had fabricated, as if pretending long enough can make something real.

The victims advised that they did hold each other and she shivered and he sobbed for what she said was a minute and he said was ten, until another vehicle, a minivan, approached the scene, saw the snapped pole in the road plus the crying couple on the berm, and came to a stop.

The driver of this vehicle was me. And although it's been nine years I've tried to join the Deliver Area Police force (or, really, any regional safety team from which I could gain the experience needed to transfer to DAP, which is my hometown force, the same force that, as you know, failed to save my mother from the house my father set on fire), and even after the online academy, after the doctor's note advised that my condition would in no way affect my ability to perform the work, I was and am not an official of the local law. I was and am, alone, my region's (population 26) community watchperson. Excuse all the background. Sgt. Jonas, I am composing myself. I was the third person. The watchperson. Not yet a policeman, but finally in the position to police. Let me start over.

I did—like a professional—pull out my pocket notepad. I waved the couple over and listened closely to their story, advising them both to be factual, trying at first to record it all shorthand, which I learned from an online course I took to show my dedication to policecraft and to beef up the resume. But I instead wrote with this sloppy hybrid cursive and capitals (which is why it's taking so long to get all this down, transcribing my own notes. Chicken Scratch, Mom used to call it), and recording more than I should, more fat than meat, maybe, but I did nod empathetically at what sounded like key details—especially the knife stabs, the hair pull, the crying, the shirt-up-over-the-male-victim's-face thing, which he still had going on, the collar drawing a line across his eyes so that I could only make contact with the upper halves. I did for some reason picture the victim smiling in there. I allowed my . . . what's the proper police word for gut-itch? (It's like how detectives in crime documentaries detail a kind of sixth sense, an internal barometer for sensing someone's truth.) My gut-itch colored the way I processed information about this male victim. Everything I tried to observe evenly felt uneven.

The victim did inquire, through his shirt, if I could please call the [expletive] police. I advised that, as the regional watchperson, I could escort them to the station. And I did pull back my black flannel to show them my t-shirt, which says (as you can see from that camera in the corner of the room) DELIVER TWP WATCH—REGION

#003. The victims stared at me blankly. I advised it was not safe to stand here. The road—you would know if you ever drove out here, Sgt. Jonas—has zero shoulder. I advised: Let's go. I smiled. Warmly. We had bonded somewhat over their honest and abundant release of incident details, and I cashed in on this trust by opening the van doors, waving them in. The victims did hesitate, conferencing quietly, until she seemed to assure him, and they climbed in. She to shotgun, he to the middle bench of my cruiser (a baby-blue, inherited Ford Windstar, which, editorial, cuts the wind like a hot spoon through freezer burn). When we rounded the corner of Baylor Rock, we charged into the forest toward justice. Or what we hoped would evolve into justice.

Sometimes justice is just coincidence with pants on. And for years it has been my daily objective to rise and put pants on, to be at the ready for today, just as Mom always demanded. It's what got me here. What put a watchperson inside a serious criminal justice event. With victims in tow, I thought about how much this was my moment—I got lost in seeing this scene from above, looking down from the sky at this watchperson in his moment. Something was missing. I stopped the van, which Dad called Petty but I named Earnhardt, and went to the trunk to retrieve my rotating amber emergency light. It was there because I had put it there, beside my taser, zip ties, and lunch box. I grabbed them all. The light suctioned tightly to the roof of Earnhardt. For years I had dreamt of using this tool, my amber light, the heads it might turn, the way it would splash the dim pines with color. It turns out the light is not so strong, but I imagined the color as we drove, and this was almost enough for me.

I wish it had been enough.

I'm sorry this report is so long. If you want to know my weakness, and I know this isn't a job interview, or even a conversation at all, but more of a—(I'm not using Sgt. Jonas's word, because Confessions are for criminals). My weakness is being unsure what's essential.

Earnhardt was quiet for three minutes. No talking. No advising. I did wonder if the victims appreciated the various sunlit hues streaming through the thicker or lighter clumps of leaves. Is this how they pictured being rescued? Did the road seem wound naturally around the Appalachian foothills or, like some car commercial, deliberately twisted? I never wanted Turtlebell to end. I followed it on and on. I felt nervous, responsible that this road was part of my home, my charge, my watch, my zone, and these poor people were taking it in without an ounce of magic, rather with pounds of terror. I looked at her. I saw him in the mirror. They did hug their doors. Finally, the female victim asked who I was.

I advised that I am the neighborhood watchperson.

She tried to make a joke, something like: That was a neighborhood?

I advised that there's a perimeter. Eleven homes in the perimeter. Years ago it was 12 homes. I informed her that my name was Lonny but please call me Officer Salter.

The victim behind me in the middle bench asked (editorial: it was kind of a whine) if we were headed to the real police. As I nodded, I felt a jolt somewhere at the top of my spine. Like remembering you left the gas stove on, the right burner, high heat, baked beans cementing to the pot. I did realize that I was driving farther and farther away from town. Deeper into forest. Out of the county, maybe. He must have known, somehow, that the police station was far behind. I heard a soft, mean sobbing, his whole head now submerged in the shirt. Was I lost? I can't say. I knew the general lay of this land, but not its every twist and shout. I advised they give me more information for my report. This to distract from the fact

I didn't know where I was driving, what I was doing. It was a car full of victims, me becoming the third. Me victimizing me. I didn't recognize these trees. I need you to take my notepad and record facts, I advised, in a low voice.

The female victim laughed. At me. Her laughter rocked her back and forth. I felt my cheeks get hot. I was missing basic info. One thing I know from my years of study: this work is about facts, so much about facts that if an officer can simply gather each clean fact the truth will radiate. Failure happens when the recorder of facts (which is all we really are, wouldn't you say, Sgt. Jonas?) forgets that they do not yet have all the facts down on paper and begins to rutch around for the meaning, the tissue and ligament and blubber that make the bones of the plot a body, a narrative. Just get everything down correctly. Such as, names—

Barbara and Richmond Salter.

Such as, medical summary—

She's diabetic and he's a fucking prick.

Such as, the address—

That night, twenty years ago, the cruisers could not find our house, kept missing the driveway, which is long and stony, a secret of the woods. You would've known where it was if you'd ever once driven out to investigate the official complaints me or Mom made about Dad's wrath and stolen pill bottles. Your dumb officers drove around the mountain while our roof burned. I did about the same amount of nothing-good as my local fire and police teams—I sat in my tree fort, watching, trying to smell the supper I had started. Don't stop reading, Jonas.

Both hands gripping the wheel, I did inquire of the victim's names. My notebook sat on the dash. She grabbed it, opened to a new page, and began to write loudly, an attack on the paper. I asked about the car, any defining features, and we entered another dense corridor of jack pine.

She wrote: Carlie Wylie and Kevin Balcome had their pale gray, '99 Honda Civic, which they call Hackett, stolen (and I had to dictate this next part because she suggested "bum [expletive] forest") at the Baylor Rock hairpin on Turtlebell Road. The car has a sticker on the back that reads: COEXIST—EXCEPT WITH NAZIS, and should have stab marks on the window.

As I did steer through the curves of Baylor Preserve, she editorialized about the perpetrator. I advised she be more hard-factual. Color of hair. Height. Eyes. Defining features. She said, quote: He's an inbred [expletive] with a shit-patch beard, grown in the waste-pit of some hick-ass meth lab. When she laughed, her gray tongue jutted from her mouth like a goat's. It was clear she was angry, and I could hear her hand shaking, the pen stabbing the paper, but my assumption was that she wanted badly to laugh. To hear laughter.

A quote: He looked like the kind of guy—Kev, wouldn't you say?—the kind of guy who feeds beer to a dog and giggles? Who blows pot smoke in a dog's face, films it on his flip phone?

The male victim pulled his shirt down for the first time and whispered to her through the square hole in the headrest. Paraphrase: Where the [expletive] are we being taken? Why hasn't he called the police? I didn't want to call you, Sgt. Jonas. This was under my control. I did again attempt to distract their attention away from me and back to the facts.

Ofc. Salter: Do you get a read on the suspect's height?

—We're really close to the party. His parents' house is nearby. You can just drop—

Ofc. Salter: We don't have time for a party. This is police work.

—Listen. Please, drop us off, and we'll call the police from there.

Ofc. Salter: You know, it's funny. How we both name our vehicles?

—We want to be taken there. (The male victim's face emerged from the shirt.)

—This is how you can help us. (The female victim said this as she reached for me.)

She put her hand on the top of my hand, which was placed on the gear shift. Did she fear I would throw the whole thing in reverse? I wish I could have. She even offered to fetch me a plate when we arrived at the party. Hot dogs. Did I like hot dogs, hot dogs and beans? I focused on the road. I forgot I was a watchperson many times. Many times it seemed like I was just me, Lonny Salter, driving Mom down the mountain for roller-tacos at Tom's Exxon. Officers, detectives—I have one question: How do you remember the mission? How do you keep your mind from letting the mission flit away, up and up, behind a cloud, only a few feathers left to collect? Is the key to being a servant of the law killing the threat of the day dream? Maybe I'm meant for something else. Fireman. Mushroom farmer. Bird dog. Jail cell.

I advised that the only truth of the moment was that we needed gas. The orange light did in fact begin to blink. The female victim motioned toward my phone in the center console, claiming she would provide directions.

No, I live here, I said, though I did not recognize anything. I had felt this sensation once before, riding home from the job interview for groundskeeper at the Deliver Area Police Station. That too had been my moment, for a moment. I'd figured: It's a job. Gotta start somewhere. So I rode there on my John Deere—do you remember, Jonas?—just to show my moxie, my mower as a resume, and I was laughed out of the interview. The officers advised me to leave. Go home, Big Guy, they said. You know where that is? Home? Were they joking? I promise I was not. I just wanted a job, or at least a chance. A three-mile ride back, but somehow I got lost. Ran out of gas. Tried to hitch. No one stopped for me.

The orange light did cease blinking altogether. Earnhardt was on fumes. The victims were silent, tense. The female victim's hands did grip the armrest (metaphorical) like a weapon.

I glanced at my cell in the cupholder, and she grabbed it before I could.

Google Maps, she said.

This is when, I believe, you first heard from her, Sgt. Jonas—she must have texted the hotline. I didn't know—she moved quick. She must have sent you the address of the Sunoco. How did she describe me? Kidnapper? Thief? Unemployable? Bystander? Late-term orphan? Stranger to his own road? Big Guy? Someone you pat on the shoulder and say Chin up, Big Guy, like he's a pet, a toddler? Criminal? Perp? Hero? Creep? Dunce? Something I haven't heard yet?

She set the phone sideways in the cupholder. I followed the blue line to the gas mart.

How to describe the silence for the next four miles. I spent the time mentally sketching the most accurate and detailed and well-lit picture of the suspect. Editorial: maybe I'm an artist. In my mind, the portrait of the perp was so textured it could talk. He said to me: Focus. You're wasting your shot. The flagger had green eyes, a lisp. Stay the course. Be justice.

Why would someone do that? What kind of person stabs another person? This was the male victim talking. His head now in his hands. I did desire to provide an answer, but I am, editorially, only a fact collector. The whys are for detectives. Right, Jonas? Why is my father not in prison?

The female victim climbed through the middle passage and joined him on the bench seat, put her hands around his shoulders. His head did remain submerged in his shirt. And I did steer off the Old Archway Road and briefly onto Lemon Hollow and into the Barney's lot, and right up to those classic (editorial: decrepit) gas pumps. The victims were seated on the middle bench. I advised I would pump just three gallons (my next SSI check still ten days away) and we'd be en route to the party. I'd meant to say police station. My hands rattled. I couldn't hold my wallet. The male victim advised he was heading inside to use the bathroom.

I did throw the power locks (they're child-proof too).

I gave an official order: Everyone stays where they are.

I pulled my Taser from my pocket and showed them how the blue spark jumps the gulf.

Exiting the car, I selected hi-test and watched the numbers climb. I surveyed my surroundings, observed the scene, meditated on its dangers. I saw the heat of the day. I tasted the sweat on my face. I saw a mother/son team climb into a truck. How easy it'd be to treat my community like a video game, to burst into the Barney's with a hard hand sticking in my coat pocket, taking all the money plus a Coke on the way out. Or just fill a bucket with Super, stroll inside, douse it all in gas—the snacks, the counter, the rollers, the donuts, and threaten to light a match if someone didn't help. I saw dark spots on the concrete below me, probably ancient gum, driven into the ground thousands of times, stains like black grease at the bottom of the pan. I leaned down and peeked in the back window, witnessed the male victim reach toward the dash.

Some field bird cawed siren-like. The passenger side window began to slide down.

I advised: Don't leave me. I reported: You're my victims.

Just then, my right hand was covered with a thick, warm fluid. The gas tank, overflowing. The meter read: $29.58. I didn't have that. Gas did pool at my feet. I couldn't release the handle. It wanted to be pulled. I was stuck in an ice block. With my other hand I clutched my taser, felt its heat in my pocket, what it wanted. I closed my eyes, waited to burst into flames.

The female victim fell out of the window, hard to her knees. She screamed. The male victim followed, full face exposed to the world. He grabbed and lifted and sort of carried her, running, limping across the lot toward the bean field. The sounds of sirens filled my ears, something I hear only when I fall asleep. I saw what it was they were escaping. I saw him too—an old Civic parked beside the dumpster, a man inside eating with a spoon.

My hand released the pump. My hand checked my pockets. Taser. Power bar. Quarter-inch zip ties perfect for a citizen's arrest. The sirens wailed louder. I moved on the suspect. I thought of the YouTube video called "How to Cuff a Perp with Zips Quick," but all I could recall was the color of the host's teeth, green in the odd yard light, one canine gone gray. The way he flipped the perp-actor, probably his brother, down into the grass and kneed his back until his victim whispered: Jesus, man you're really hurting me.

The suspect in the Civic, he sat up straight. He saw me coming. He would flee. I was running. The sirens were coming from somewhere inside me. But the suspect, a father, was not alone. Mom in shotgun, kids in back. They passed around a pint of ice cream. When I saw that the car was a Focus, not a Civic, I should have stopped dead, stranded myself in the center of the parking lot, my moment over, my victims long gone, but I couldn't get in the way of my own momentum. I pounded the passenger window. Excuse me, ma'am. Let me in. Take me with you. Take my weapon. Fire. Put a blue jolt through me. Fire. Jonas, can't you tell the rest? You were there by then, you and your heroes, slamming doors, taking positions, watching it all through the sights of your pistols, shouting any name you thought belonged to me.

ETERNAL NIGHT
AT THE NATURE MUSEUM,
A HALF-HOUR DOWNRIVER FROM
THREE MILE ISLAND

On the roof grows a tree Facilities kills every summer. Killed, rather. As the men from Facilities are gone. As everyone—staff, faculty, public—is gone, gone for what Harrisburg still calls temporary. The museum belongs to no one now. Or rather, belongs to that tree, or to the animals and their chewed-through glass, or to the time we lost a snake, every time we lost a snake we couldn't find for days and stayed open for visitors anyway. What I mean is the museum belongs to, I don't know, some kid? The one I sensed hiding in every building I ever closed down for the night. The same kid I imagined stowing away inside the tree trunk, or the shark's mouth, or the trash tote in the mop closet—this milk-mouthed kid with nothing to lose, too spooked to say uncle after having chosen hiding, now living out what was never a Disneyland fantasy but rather the lesser of two let-downs. Life, alone in a building full of owl eggs, appeal letters, revisionist archaeology, and arctic wolves who leap like puppies, glass eyes gleaming through their taxidermy. The building belongs to, yes, this starved sapling of a person. And the minute the kid finishes the fish food, cracks two teeth on hematite, retches up the crickets, licks all the pollen from the dead bees' legs—the climbing begins. Up stairs. Up stories. Learning from the lizards who clawed away their cages, this kid will bore with whittled obsidian and patience a hole through the third-floor utility door. Behind which lies the ladder, and so, the roof. And so, the tree. And so, the fruit.

STAY, GO

In Jersey, we did neither.

My boyfriend and I just rode the elevator. At the Hampton all weekend, we pranked guests, conducted social experiments, collected data we never wrote down. Facing the wall, backs to the elevator doors, we challenged anyone to join us in our error. Our metrics: How many people would turn to stand like us? How long until they flipped? How many seconds until everyone in the elevator stood backward like us runaways? Most turned immediately. We hid our faces. If the audience asked questions, we kept silent. That's what Marco called everyone else but me: audience. Only once did someone try to correct us—an outlier, meaningless, but I remember her French tips, zebra stripes, the knock her stilettos made on the marble. *Son,* she whispered, *turn around.* I pulled a glossy paper bird from my pocket, handed it to her, and said, *Shhhhh.*

What waited in our room was a big bleach stain on the carpet—a mistake in my makeover, and it stank. Marco pinched me some glasses from the hotel bar and my disguise was complete. Now I was a man—astute, escaped, sixteen, free, my blond hair leaning a little green—who looked nothing like the photo of the boy on the news. They said I'd been missing for two days, but we didn't like that term. Missing. Was there a word for somewhere between *lost* and *found*?

⌇

We never left the Hampton. We camped in the elevator, where we could feel what the streets of Newark offered, but feeling was enough—the long breath of possibility, a little fear, a little hope, even that faint, foul scent of crab. We held on to that. We lingered. If we hung out in the room at all it was for sex, or showers, or we passed time coloring each other's hair and folding the pages of porn into origami. These were skills I believed, somehow, someday, might come in handy—patience, focus, how to see a line before it's there. I made animals; Marco, aircraft. I loved him. He had dark, wide, stubborn hair I could pin down into braids and dye individually. His dreads looked like Nerds Rope. Nights, I toyed with those cords until he slept and then penned muddled, unsendable letters to my mother on hotel stationery.

Marco's favorite act—we called it *The No You*—was where we'd stand as close as possible to the doors, a few other passengers behind us, and wait for the elevator to open on the lobby. Then, one of us would motion for the other to go first. *No, you,* the other would say.

Oh, but I insist.

You're so polite, but seriously, it's all you.

No, you.

You.

You!

Eventually the people waiting behind us would angle their way out, hurrying past before the doors trapped everyone in. We kept a timer. The record was set when the doors closed and not a single person had left. Together we rode right back up—all of us.

I laughed so hard Marco had to hold me.

We never agreed on much, but we were firm in our belief that the

true draw of a hotel was its elevator. Tight space, dim light, the lottery of who will join that awkward, heavy quiet. The elevator is the
trip. The elevator means you're almost there. It's almost sex, almost
dinner, almost show, museum, zoo, almost sleeping spread wide
as a starfish. Almost a scalding shower, almost a cab ride. In an
elevator there's not much to do except be alive around each other.
Most just look at their shoes, or their phones (we'd ditched ours for
fear of tracking), or those glowing buttons. If you're brave you can
look at other people's faces—you're allowed—but no one does. If
you're us, you can hand them a horse folded out of porn. We were
romantic in that way, in our need to unseam social norms. We were
whispering our message: the whole essence of travel is distilled into
middle spaces. Empty moments. Though common knowledge says
an elevator is for people with a place to go, we said no. We rode over
and over and over.

Our place to be right now was here.

Marco had come into some money the day he turned eighteen,
two weeks earlier, something about a second uncle who had, for
a brief and litigious time, been mayor of the city of Orlando. We
didn't know what we were doing in Newark, or anywhere. We were
working through it at the Hampton. Sometimes we ordered room
service cocktails, but we never went into bars to use our fake IDs.
By Sunday, it'd been three days at that hotel. We sat on the win-
dow-side loveseat in our room like, Okay, let's figure this out: We
can go north. A ton of cheap land in Maine. We could try Canada,
where health insurance is a right. We could go home and kill our
parents, haha. But for Marco, that meant central Florida, where his
mom lived. He shook his head.

"Okay," I said. "Seriously, let's make a plan."

Marco laughed and flew his porno plane—smack—into the window.

The origami I obsessed over that weekend was this bird called a swallow. It's a bitch because you have to unfold the whole thing completely just to get a final crease in the beak. You spend half an hour crafting and then you have to take each piece apart to finish. My hands would shake like the hotel was coming down. *Chill out,* Marco would murmur. *I'm really trying,* I'd say.

Instead of a plan, we spent Sunday afternoon devising new ruses. We returned to the elevator, dragging in a chair from our room. I wore a dress and sat with a magazine in my lap. When the box was full of people in severe heels, hairspray, and luminescent dresses, it began. Marco entered in a bathrobe fashioned as a lab coat, holding a clipboard he'd nabbed from the front desk. He placed a hand on my shoulder and my whole body raced with anticipation. Then, he spoke with a deep, doctorly, bedside manner: "Ma'am, we have the results."

"Oh god," I sighed. "Give it to me straight." I forgot to mention I was wearing my Lady Gaga wig—white-blond with those goddess bangs—the one I used on the getaway drive from Pennsylvania. I'd taken to sleeping with it on, even though we'd cut and dyed my hair to hell.

Marco took a deep breath, put a hand on my shoulder, and said, "You're a homosexual."

Here I sobbed on cue.

That night I learned of my talent for crying on command. All I had to do was conjure up my mother's face thinking about my face. I bawled until the lenses of my glasses fogged.

Marco asked the passengers to pray for me. As the elevator doors pulled open, someone clapped, ruining everything. I threw the wig on the floor. We wanted to create discomfort, not entertainment. We didn't understand that they were the same thing.

I think that what Marco and I truly wanted was to be in that box when the machine got stuck between floors, to be trapped and not at fault for it, to have men in yellow uniforms pry open the doors and pull us to safety. At least—I think—that's what I wanted.

So, that night, we rode the elevator into morning. But something was off. Waking up in a Hampton on a Monday would feel, just, wrong. The hotel loses all its cachet if there's no next destination. How do you savor the middle if there is no end? You only crease the page because you know it will be a bird. Plus, honestly, how much of Marco's money were we going to spend on these games? We'd had three days to figure it out.

We paced the eight-by-eight box of the Hampton's elevator #3. No one else was getting on. The sun—you could see it from the eighteenth-floor window each time the doors slid open—had begun to bubble above the skyline, and that's when a security guard walked into the elevator.

"I've heard about you two," he said. His uniform was too small and his tattoos showed.

Marco immediately began speaking in Spanish (*Vete, audiencia!*). I did some quasi-ASL, random gestures, eventually moving my fingers like scissors, pantomiming slicing off my ears.

"So you're artists," he said, ripping the wig from my head. "An artist worth ten thousand dollars." Then he had Marco by a braid. "An artist worth a long sentence for kidnapping a minor."

The elevator stopped. The doors weren't opening. He killed his squawking radio.

Marco promised to dye the guard's hair any color he wanted. I offered an origami dog. Then a blowjob.

Marco laughed but looked at me sideways like, *How much of this is a joke?* My offer hung there in the air, and as the door parted open, the guard smiled.

Marco shoved him hard, and we flew, swooping into the dark city like bats.

Growing up I learned something I don't think most kids know, which is that the best part of a vacation is before it ever starts. That preceding day and a half when the thing feels finally here, when you're packing, singing, making plans for classmates to collect your worksheets—the restless sleep you take on the eve of the drive. Nothing, not even the first turn in the road, the first stop at Sunoco, the first rip in a bag of Sun Chips, nothing yet has ended. No one is screaming. Neither parent has had *Enough.* The single ticket flight back to Pennsylvania is still unbooked. A jellyfish has not yet stung you. A stranger is not pissing on your hand.

What I mean is the night Marco came for me—sleeping in the backyard on the broken trampoline, the black vinyl bed sagging into the wet grass—was the best day of my life.

That restless sleep contained every part of the world.

I remember I woke to the rattling of springs, terrified.

After the guard, we switched hotels. The Marriott was no destination, but there we were, stuck in another interim space. These elevators had A/C, colored lights, and the weirdest thing ever: doors on either side of the compartment. You'd reach a floor and have to guess which set would open. It unnerved me.

But then Marco discovered how, at the top floor, both doors opened at once. The new plan was to stand outside the elevator, and when those doors slid open: run, leap, clear the empty elevator completely. I tried to imagine us landing firm-footed in the opposite lobby.

We stood on the twenty-fourth story and waited for the bell to ding. For our path to open. For the double row of doors to unfold like a swallow.

And when they did, we saw straight through to the other side.

You, he said.

No, you, I mean it.

SPIT IF YOU CALL IT FEAR

Waylon still ain't over Y2K.

He's my brother and I love him but, Jesus, I won't miss him.

His canned goods stockpile is so big and silver in his backyard you can see it from Google Maps. He tears off all the labels on account of food is food, so it's just can after can, stacked two tall, running in rows from the edge of the woods up to the porch of the home we grew up in. The underground shelter he dug is packed with bottles of Nestlé water—you know, the cheap shit, tastes like pipe.

"That's how life's gonna taste anyway," he likes to tell me, "when it all zeroes out."

He's yet to invite me, or anyone else, into his postapocalypse fantasy—all this prepping's all for him, his private Independence Day.

Or at least that's how it seemed until today, when I come with him canning. He won't answer my check-up calls, so the only way to talk to him is to help with some project. So we're out behind Aldi's with a black trash bag for full cans, a white one for empties. Waylon's up on the dumpster, about to hop inside, but then he stops, pats his ass pocket, pulls out his cellular.

"Mom calling?" I ask. He's just standing up there, balancing on the edge, staring at the technology. A doc who's asked daily to stop practicing medicine—that's what Way looks like to me. It's the beige trench jacket, like a surgeon's stained lab coat, his big bottle glasses with the left lens cracked. Those muttonchops got wild since his reenactor days.

He was eccentric even as a teen, all hopped up on our dad's doomsday theories. But Waylon will forever be a head taller, three years older, and tenfold braver than me. I always listen when he speaks.

"You think she's the only person I talk to?" he says, glaring down at me.

"Know full well she is." He's afraid of people, though he spits if you call it fear—more like nobody's worthy of his trust. He's a loner. MacGyver. Three clicks batshit. Always armed.

"Well," he says, pecking out a text message. "Wrong!"

What we'll do with the used aluminum is haul it all to Waylon's place, where he'll melt it in his backyard forge and fashion thin pieces of armor—lightweight and wearable and, to his mind, resistant to electricity. Waylon's future's got blue bolts of man-made lightning leaping across the plain like antelopes, galloping toward all of our homes and bodies, hot for a place to rest. It was supposed to happen on Y2K, but things've been delayed. 2038—now *that's* the year the computers are set to lose their shit, Waylon says, something about a hiccup with the date change, Earth's tilt, 32-bit systems, binary's going to break. The world's set to enter something called the Trinary period, where all computer systems and electrical programs will have to adapt to a new code with three numbers—zero, one, *and* two. And like every in-between period in history, the sure-as-shit result will be a ton of pain. Unrest. A power grid that becomes, itself, a critter species, roaming all of the terrestrial US. Rivers becoming charged. Whole oceans. The rain'll snap and glow with current, Christmas lights tossed down from heaven.

I always tell Waylon he should make a website, spread the word, who knows who you can find. Partners. A militia. Company. But he hates anything with a screen, which is why I'm half-spooked to see his eyes holding contact with the cell phone.

"Who is it then?" I ask him. "Who you texting?" He's inside the dumpster now and I'm just outside, talking through the green metal barrier. He tosses out an empty Progresso.

"Deb," he says. "Met her on Prepper."

"Prepper?"

"Prepper," he says, poking his head up from the dumpster, handing me a half-drank High Life tallboy. "It's a dating application."

"For nutbars?" I say.

"For realists, shit. Deb claims to have the state's largest supply of dryer lint."

"Very realistic," I say. Mom is convinced Way's gonna end up in prison. *You have to help your poor brother see the real world.* "I mean, dryer lint. Damn."

"It's for fires, shitbird. Lights quicker than leaves, burns hotter than a newspaper."

"Bullshit," I say. "But are you two fucking or what?" I say, trying to make it so we're teens again, and this tallboy's in my hand not because I need the aluminum but because I downed it in one long gulp in a race against my brother. But we're not seventeen. We're murky in our thirties. And what do we have to show for it? I mean, at least Waylon has a project. That's the sad part. My only purpose has been monitoring my brother to give Mom peace and working at Little Caesars long enough each month to afford rent and Jack and bait. And I don't even really like fishing. I just like watching the water, the easy, quiet passing of time. The rest of the world's just too fast—the work rush, the phone screen, the shit I see behind my eyes when I won't sleep. It all feels like whiplash. Swear to God, the millennium was yesterday.

So, I fish. Or more like I just sit. To be true, it's a pain when something bites the line. Because then you have to act.

"You two gonna take off, get hitched in Vegas?" I add.

"Shit, Greg, who's got time for that?" he says. "And I ain't even met Deb in person yet. Which is why I'm tickled you're here, actually. I'm fixing to head over to her trailer, see if this stash is all she talks it up to be."

I came out with my brother today to tell him I got to go. There's work I found on an offshore ship, out in Alaska. You live belowdecks, work fifteen-hour days, let the icy rain beat you into a man or else kill you. That's why the pay's so high—death rate is military grade. There was no interview. You just need all your limbs. They could care less if you cooked a hundred thousand pizzas and held a job for eight years. Hell, you could be a felon. All you have to be is there. Reliable. And no one can call me unreliable, but I am reaching some place past tired.

Sheila at work is always saying, "Day in and day out." *Scrubbing the oven, day in and day out.* But I never once felt a day go out. It's always day in and day in. *Day in, day in.* Grease and cheese. *Day in, day in.* One night you get robbed, *Day in, day in, day in.*

On the drive over to Deb's my hopes go up. If she seems adult enough, maybe I can put my brother in her care. Waylon's got no friends. Most of Gettysburg knows him, finds him unsavory. Even the conspiracy theorists who hang around the sword store have cut him out of their circle whole-hog for begging cans and blankets off them. Mom rarely gets to leave Battlefield Assisted Care, so she only checks up on Way via phone. He rarely answers, afraid of what the waves do to his brain, so most often she checks up on him via me. Wait'll she hears about this Deb woman.

We're heading long into the woods, and it's nice, green, everything wet. I roll the window down and breathe, looking up at the canopy. Way and I used to play in the woods plenty, but we never thought about putting stakes down. Thing about nature is we all know it's the secret but we're just too brainwashed to make a change. Shit, Deb, you did it right.

And maybe I have too, you know, maybe Alaska really is my destiny. I still can't picture myself on the boat, honestly, but I've got the email telling me to come. Pack light and buzz your hair is some of their advice. Report to port in two weeks. Everything happens all at once.

Thank God for how Way steers around the bends even-steven, no sudden shit, no visions, and damn, his newest pills must be working. The hills of south Adams County dip down into a valley—doesn't feel like Maryland yet, but the border's here somewhere—and a shape starts to come into focus. With my eyes closed, I swear I see the hull of my ship pulling through the fog.

"Wake up, Greg," Waylon says. We're pulled off to the shoulder. "Need you alert here."

"I think she seems like a perfect match," I say, half-asleep.

"Brother, we ain't even there yet. House is down the road a ways—but let me warn you," he says, "about preppers." A cloud of mosquitoes hovers outside my window. "Preppers only look out for themselves. Understand?" He honks the horn. "Scenario: she says she wants to meet, but in fact she's got a man hiding in her bathroom, locked and loaded, ready to kidnap me the second I step foot in her trailer. What he does then is shoots you in the toe to show he's serious. Ties me up. Throws me in the back of a truck, pulls the bed cover over so I'm trapped back there, limps your ass to the passenger's seat, speeds off, demands with a gun to your head that you show them where my place is at, and you're a pussy so you take them right there no problem. And then Deb holds a gun to your head as the man raids my backyard of cans. They dig a hole and throw us both in it. They set fire to the house and the land it lives on—mind you, this is our house, our father's house, Mom's land, which belonged to her granddad, the very place where we were raised and reared—and we die, and they make off with my food and my water."

"I thought you stopped watching movies," I say.

"Doesn't mean I can't see a plot," he says. "But hey," he pats my knee like Dad used to do before saying something sarcastic. "At least we'll burn together, right?"

But the irony's not coming across.

Deb's trailer is painted camo. Just a hell of a job.

"Smart move, woman," Waylon says. We idle in her gravel drive. He hasn't gotten out of the truck. My brother reaches over to the glovebox in front of me and clicks the button. It falls open, and there's two pistols.

"No, sir," I say.

"Jesus, are you still jacked up about the burglary?"

"It was a robbery, and no, I—"

"Oh, right," Way says, "you went and gave him everything he asked for—cash, cheese sticks, wristwatch, your fucking shoes . . ." It's a classic talk from Way. Him ripping into me over *my* life choices, like he's our dad. "You need to learn how to hold one of these, anyway," he says, setting the gun on my leg. "For safety. Help me here. Remember the plot?"

I put the gun back in the glovebox. "I'll be here, in the truck," I say. "If anything goes down, I'll back you up. They won't even know I'm here." I crouch low in the floor space. "See," I say, peeking up, "nobody can see me." But through the windshield I spot a woman on the little metal front porch. Her hair is a puffy red cloud around her head, and she's got some kind of giant scarf draped across her shoulders. She waves at us. Her eyes are green as the center of the sea.

The two eyes were all I saw, stone black as a salamander's. It was three months back they hit the Little Caesars, but again, everything feels like yesterday. I don't know if it was a man, woman, or teenager. They shot a bullet in the menu board above my head and opened a backpack. Eyes spoke. Mouth never said a word. The bag waited on the counter, wanting more. Later, the police would demand details, descriptors, calling me a liar, but all I could give them was the eyes. I think the black ski mask had an orange burn mark, like someone left it too long on a woodstove, but I don't know, I could've made that up. There was no time to think. They wouldn't leave until the bag was filled. Our cash wasn't enough. I shook, man, I put my shoes in. My watch. Food. I kept moving, filling. You sit still long enough, someone's bound to come and knock you down.

With a gun tucked in the ass of his jeans, Waylon marches up to the home of Deb, the lint lord.

"You didn't tell me you were bringing a friend!" she calls as he stomps through the muddy gravel. "I've got Lay's and queso, but that's about all."

Waylon pulls the pistol and orders her against the house. She obeys. Like Van Damme, he puts his back to trailer's siding, beats the front door with his fist, and sweeps inside. It all happens too fast. His moves are swift, controlled, and though I don't understand it, I'm kind of proud of him. He looks like a hero should. Through the windows, I can see him checking each room, weapon out ahead of him. It seems the gun is what's moving, and he's only following it.

I hop out the truck and tiptoe up to the side of the trailer, right beside Deb.

"I'm sorry," I say. "I don't know why he's like this."

"I do," she says. "And it's goddamn smart." She smells fresh as laundry. "If a guy can't perform a proper safety sweep, honey, that's a burning red flag."

"I'm not even supposed to be here," I say. Why not practice on Deb? Maybe she can help me break the news to Way. "I have a job waiting in Alaska."

"Then why ain't you in Alaska?" she says.

"Plane leaves tomorrow."

"Then why ain't you packing? Tell me: On a map, do you even know where Alaska's at?"

Deb's looking both at and past me, like she clearly sees the shock I felt when I found, last night on the internet, a graphic of Alaska superimposed over the rest of the US. Shit you not—go look this up—it stretches from the east coast all the way to the west.

Growing up on the edge of the woods, we were told by our father we could do what we wanted, as long as we looked out for each other. He said this mostly to me, being it was always my eye contact he had. Waylon was older by three years, but when I entered school, he was still in my grade. Sometimes in Mrs. Marina's class, trying to read a Hardy Boys book aloud, I'd hear Waylon in the hallway, laying into a teacher. Later, when he was on Behavioral Ed track and in a different building, I swear I could still hear him hollering if the classroom window was open.

I tried to look out for Waylon, but he was bigger and in a lot of ways sharper. In the woods I'd point out things like maybe we shouldn't cross here—*the water looks high*—but that never stopped him, and we'd get through fine. *Old Man Greene owns this land, maybe we should scram*—but he'd carve his name into a tree. And, of course, I'd help him get all the letters right.

The last time Dad said to watch out for each other, I was sixteen. It was early December, 1999, and Dad was leaving to protest the federal government. His theory supposed they'd not only engineered the coming disaster called Y2K, but they were keeping us taxpayers in the dark about the true degree of havoc on its way. My mother and him fought like crows over roadkill, screaming and flapping and ugly. But he went. He left us. He said he was fighting for the future. We never saw him again.

Waylon believes he's a hero, because he stopped Y2K, at least for the time being. To escape the grip of the government agents after him, Dad went dark, off-grid, gone. On rosier days he talks about Dad living strong in a community of outlaws, working to stop what's still on the horizon: any kind of Armageddon. But when Way gets bent, he loses confidence that Dad has the grit to fend them off forever. "He's got no one to look out for him," he told Mom and me one night over Chinese food at the home. "Any day now, he could fall, and we'll be doomed. There's no way he can make it all the way to 2038." I kept eating—silence helps his delusions to sink back down beneath the surface. Mom put her head in her hands, like there was something shaking loose and she was trying to keep it intact, something she couldn't let Waylon and me see, or know.

After that, Mom, who's sick in her own ways, made me swear to keep Waylon out of trouble. Now both parents have forced this promise onto me. Today, I live a mile from Waylon and his canned goods stockpile, but I swear, some nights, with the window of my apartment open, I can hear him screaming at a radio, firing bullets into the face of a television.

"Clear!" Waylon yells, and then reemerges through the front door. Deb and I both peel ourselves from the side of the trailer. The paint's still kind of wet and sticks to my cheek.

"What do you think of the place?" Deb asks my brother.

"You know," he says, putting the gun back in his pants. "The shitter's real spacious."

"You're not lying. In most single-wides, your knees push right up against the door." They laugh. Deb's scarf, I notice now, is dryer lint, woven. Maybe she is, in fact, the real deal.

"Waylon Bens," says my brother, holding out a hand to shake.

"Deborah Arlington." But she hugs him. "So I hear your brother's moving to Russia."

Waylon laughs, then Deb joins him, and I smile as big as I can but nothing comes out.

"No, you got the wrong man," Way says, the sun both above us and in his eyes. His right lens is cracked now too. "Greg can't move away. I promised Daddy I'd always look after him."

Sometimes I wish I'd been the one born a little nuts. Seems there's some benefit. It's an automatic reason for any action you take (you're Waylon, you know, that's just what you do). There's such careful attention your family pays to your every word, every day you survive. You have no conscience or hang-ups about being exactly who, in your heart, you are.

But I suppose the downside is you can't disappear too easy. If Way took off for Alaska, we'd be after him, or I sure would, with Mom in my ear from the home. We'd call the police, like we did the last time he disappeared for a week and they found him building a lean-to on somebody's lakefront property, and that somebody surprised him with a shotgun. If he left, I'd be sent on search and rescue, showering in truck-stop bathrooms, clapping sink water in my pits. Now, if I take off alone, my family might hurt, but they won't lift a finger to find me, the traitor. I wonder if I should devise a big trick, a great lie for my leaving, something like what Dad did.

I found that fucker online last month. He never went to DC. He just goddamn left. Never believed a lick of the Y2K shit. Lives somewhere near Juneau. Bearded, dating, he sells PC parts for cheap. He brews beer, posts pictures online. Asshole called his last batch *Adams County Ale.*

I blame him to hell and back, but still, isn't what I want the same thing? The difference is, I'm set on telling them—Waylon and Mom—exactly what I'm doing, where I'm going.

Deb and Waylon, they duck inside the trailer in a gust of conversation. I head back to the truck, reach my hand down between the cracks of the seat for my phone. I dial Mom.

Waylon yells out from the trailer, "Greg, there's two bedrooms in here, man!"

And then Deb: "Yeah, we'll only have use for the one!"

Twelve rings before the ward secretary picks up. "Room number?"

"210."

Then it's hardly half a ring before she answers. "What's wrong? Waylon?"

"It's Greg, Mom," I say, pacing the gravel driveway. "And we're fine. We're both fine." From the open window of the trailer, I can hear him saying, over and over: *Oh my God.* I'm guessing Deb's showing him the lint collection. Bet it's breathtaking. In fact, I'm going to

decide it fucking is. I'm deciding right now that what each of these people have is everything the other could've hoped for, tenfold.

"Wii bowling is about to—Greg? You said he's fine? I think you're breaking up."

"I mean, yeah, Waylon's fine, Mom. He is. Him. But me, Mom, I'm, I—well," and I step into the middle of a brown puddle. But I do not drown. "I have to go somewhere soon."

"To work? Or over to Waylon's? Don't tell me you're going out fishing again. Last time we didn't hear from you for two days."

"To Alaska, Mom. I'm leaving. Tomorrow."

"Oh—Gregory David, if this is about your father," she says, all relaxed, like it's nothing, like she's just giving a stranger directions. "It's a lost cause." Behind her I hear bowling pins falling down. I know it's just digital pins, pixels on a screen, ones and zeroes, but it sounds like the real deal, like a big wave crashing.

"You know about Dad?" I ask. "You know where he is?"

"I've known, I've known. Bastard sends money every so often. Who do you think paid for Way's trailer? I didn't want to upset you boys. What with Way sure to flip out, and you fit to spend another month in bed, lose your job, and—"

The phone falls from my hand, goes black beneath the puddle. I don't reach for it. Instead, I hop onto the bed of Way's truck, pull off my wet shoe, and peel down my soaked sock. Behind me, the woods wear their purple dark in silence. Ahead, Deb's camouflage sanctuary is lit up gold and green, and there's music. I don't see the two of them inside, or anywhere, until: Jesus, there it is—a shadow on the kitchen wall that looks, for a second, like someone being held hostage. An elbow cocked, a skull, a trembling.

But when they move into the light of the window, it's just a dance. They're dancing. He's terrible. His eyes are closed. She's teaching him to trust another person. He's teaching me to trust my convictions, to live in exactly the way I see the world. Or at least he's trying, and maybe he has been forever. I close my eyes too. And whatever it is I see back behind my eyelids, it's not Alaska, and it's not Dad—but it sure as hell ain't Gettysburg, either. I slide my bare foot into my shoe and wave goodbye, whether he sees me out here in the dark or not.

SEVEN CORNERS, PENNSYLVANIA—

—a town so small we all had the same therapist, honest, and called her by her first name: Carla. Predawn in a Denny's booth, we debriefed our sessions, shared notes, compared diagnoses, and wondered where her tattoos were hidden. We marveled over Carla's insight. Her ambient charm. Her bad jazz mixes. The slight dent in her forehead, how it hued and curved the light.

We drove ourselves in circles telling stories of how she saved our lives. Where else are myths made but in dark diner corners? That long bulb flickering overhead. Gaunt faces reflected in the glass. Stomachs dumb with syrup. Waitresses tamping down our every simple need. Please, it's the cradle of conspiracy.

"She says I'm sensitive because of how I notice shit," Jed was saying. "Like those tree branches that grow over the road and sort of swallow the power line? Well, when the tree dies, and they trim it, they have to, like, leave that bit of branch up there, wrapped around the wire. Just a chunk of wood strung up like a charm on a necklace. Well, Carla noticed that I notice shit like that."

"Does Carla ever speak to you about yourself in the third person?" I asked my tablemates.

"She says I'm all about the physical world," Jed went on. "She says I hold it dear."

∽

The whole front face of her office building was coated with green hearts—morning glories, invasive and gorgeous. Sadly, by the time I arrived Monday evenings, the flowers had all gone shy and shut. The building was frigid, but her office held a dry heat. Though she saw adults, Carla's professional focus was kids, so she kept a collection of Hot Wheels on her hard carpet. Feet and feet of orange plastic track I fiddled with as I whined, feeling unjudged but unloved.

"You talk often of this lacking," she said one session that autumn, her restless, shoeless foot tapping the rug. "Would you say it's a lack of identity, a lack of meaning, or a lack of, let's call it, belonging?"

"I'm belonging fine," I said, calling to mind the diner, how the butter dollop on the Belgian waffle looked exactly like a scoop of vanilla. "But the other—what did you call it?"

"Identity?"

"I'm not sure what that one means." I slid a toy Trans Am into an orange turn.

"Present for you?" Carla said, and my goosebumps grew. "A dictionary."

I laughed. "I'll ask Santa in December."

"Sal, take me back to that moment in the shop," she said. "The morning the needle went into your wrist."

Every tailor makes mistakes. Your hands get scarred. But the thing on my wrist is scary and different and still red and the reason I first sought out the help of someone who would turn out to be her. To be Carla. I was hemming a dress pant, something simple, almost mindless, like the way you drive home without thinking once about your hands on the wheel, but my arm just kept moving toward the feed dogs, those bars of teeth that flank the needle. Closer. Closer. Until it was in me. And in me. And in me again through the backhand side of wrist.

"Doesn't everyone have those thoughts? The thing where like, you're driving over the river, and you wonder for a second how long it would take to hit the water? You know, if you just threw the wheel hard to the right?"

"Except," she said, "that is just a thought. Our thoughts are not our selves, Sal."

"Yes, at first. But that day at the machine, the thought started *happening* to me."

The blood ruined so many clothes, all of which belonged to other people.

At Denny's we fussed over Christmas, which gift to all chip in and get her. Year one was a card full of lottery tickets, but it grew to jewelry, and then that last year: a jacuzzi. No shit. Jones knew a guy who got us a used one for a song. I sewed the bow. It was 1999. We were in a bad way, brains curdled by the promise of Y2K. What could our money mean, really, after it all melted to zeroes in some billionaire's server? Love was our only material. Sausages, waffles, all this love. And you were a liar if you didn't love her.

Jones was a liar if you didn't know how to handle his hoaxes. He claimed Carla invited him over for a soak in the tub as a thank you. With him and Jed it came to blows almost, over my Moons Over My Hammy. It was a story. Jones's visit hadn't happened. *Merry Christmas,* I offered her every appointment that January, but Carla never acknowledged the gift we'd had delivered. None of us six would ever use the jacuzzi, would ever know if she used it, or what she wore when she did if she did. Not that our obsession was sexual—for everyone except for Jed, this thing was well beyond physical. Rumor was, anyway, that she sold it.

Besides, Rule One was no touching. Carla was anti-hug, kept a professional distance that was to be respected. Rule Two was born the sad night Thin Bill whispered all ten digits of her home phone number over his plate of wet eggs. When the old man protested, he was asked to leave the group and took up residence at the Denny's bar instead, until he left Denny's, and then Seven Corners, and for all we know, the earth itself, altogether.

It was an unspoken truth that our rules attempted to make what we were doing not *right*, but not illegal.

"I've been thinking about Sal's obsession with pancakes," she said one session that winter, after I'd dodged again the details of growing up with my grandfather. We often spoke about me as if I were on TV, and it turned the good blood in my head loud. "His need for something endless."

I envied the way her work consumed her, as mine had when I was tailoring in town, before the accident happened and it got so I couldn't pay the electric bill and had to close, had to find scratch work sewing repairs for the York Little Theatre costume shop. My wife, Adie, pleaded that I get help because something in me was misfiring, and I couldn't do a lick of work without pacing around the playhouse, needle and thread in hand, mistakes piling up and over.

"Sal—did you think your grandfather would let you live with him forever?" And here was Carla, sitting before me every week, a person whose work poured from her like sap—she had tapped the tree of life. She had made herself happen. I used to wonder whether she ever looked back at her past, and, if she did, was it divorced from fear, a cold object just hanging there?

Adie called the obsession unhealthy. But she saw Carla too, and after a gin and a half her love would slip out in curious questions and what-if scenarios. "What do you think happened to her head?" None of us were adult. Pushing forty, yes, but not adult in the way America demands, not grown enough for the five-day work week or the silent, God-fearing community of Seven Corners. The realtor had said the schools were beautiful. We never did get around to kids.

"Is there a lot of sax when you're in session?" Adie asked. "Is that what jazz is? Does it ever seem like she's just making shit up? Oh God—what if she stops taking Medicare?"

"You could sell your eggs," I guessed. "I'll sell sperm. I hear there's money in plasma."

Ice and all, Adie gulped her drink empty. "Kiss me," she said, lime pulp clinging to her top lip. "And promise you won't go out for breakfast tonight."

But I was already pulling on my boots.

"You're getting worse, Sal."

"Please," I said, rubbing my wrist. "How am I getting worse?"

"By not getting better."

"They can't understand," Simon said, pointing his fork at an invisible woman in the middle of the table. "God bless them, but they don't get it."

"Our wives want to teach us yoga, but Carla wants to teach us hope," said Orrin, a bitter news reporter whose wife had long left him. It would be a month before Adie did the same to me. Each of the women in our lives, God save them, would abandon her brave campaign to reconnect spiritually. We'd come home wrung out and stuck to the loveseat like gum, chewed and pale, only to flee again at ten for pancakes that slid happily from their stacks, fantasies spread thick across the corner table. A Caribbean cruise with Carla. A book club with Carla. A flight where Carla saves a planeful of passengers from something fierce on the wing. There were times too we sat in silence, bloated and confused, more than a little disappointed Y2K had never come with its ungodly eraser to even us all out.

The night Carla entered the Denny's was one of those nights.

She knew I spent a lot of time in diners, but of course our club was hush-hush (we used a booth tucked away from view of the doors, back by the bathrooms). I saw Carla climb out of a car, the passenger's seat, her dress purple as the night.

"Orrin," I said. "We got a Code Rose."

Inside her office, there were picture frames still filled with stock photos. Our little club would theorize where it was she'd come from, what it was she had left. None of us had ever seen a car that could be Carla's in the parking lot. How did she get there? How would she ever leave?

She screamed at us sometimes. "I'm not some witch! I can't just cast a spell—this shit requires your effort!" Call it tough love. She made us stand and pace as we talked, to stave off stagnation. "Move! Go!" The way her neck vein popped. We ate it up. You wouldn't understand. We didn't get it ourselves. We didn't even realize that it was wrong to pour the kind of attention you craved for yourself at the feet of any person kind enough to look you in the eye. Our behavior was sick—it's no feat to admit it. I regret every minute of the Carla years. But at that time—and this is what I can't escape—I thought what I felt was alive. Almost divine. Life had not snapped to attention like that since I was twenty-three, when my grandpa, whose abuse bred in me my fear of freedom, gripped me by the arm a final time and said, *You've got to get out and make your own life.*

✳

Things changed the night she came into Denny's. Before the waters were even on her table, Carla, our collective's private guru, had to use the bathroom.

"It's Sal—" she said in passing, but then stopped herself, choking a little on the *l*. Her legs stiffened like a charley horse was coming on. Maybe saying hello would have been some kind of malpractice. But she registered us, registered our existence, registered us with her neck muscles. She knew in an instant what we were, in that booth. Jed waved. Her right foot wobbled as she turned the corner. While she was in there, we escaped, but not unscathed. At least not I. After this breach, so many rules seemed no longer to apply to me, or at least not to Sal.

"It's just illegal," Adie would say, "or it fucking should be, the way you worship this woman."

A god she was not, but a prophet, possibly. I always saw Carla as more of a seer than an overseer. She divined this clear path I traced and traced with words. Healthy habits. Gratitude journal. A mile every morning. "No treadmill, either. What Sal needs is the out-fucking-side." Hobbies, hobbies. Dinner made with things that grew, and chewing slow, no TV in bed. A sex life with my wife like we had in '95. Carla taught me the word *intention*. The word *curvature*. The word *care*. She gave me a list of museums in nearby cities, and I went alone, daydreaming my therapist beside me. *What is this thing here? This pile of bark, what do you think it means?*

"New necklace?" I asked at my next appointment after the Denny's sighting, an appointment which Carla had rescheduled twice. She never wore the presents we purchased, and this piece around her neck was wild, shining like nothing did. "What's that stone—peridot?"

"We're going to focus on your—"

"Topaz?" I flicked a red Corvette down the track, and it flipped when the path bent left.

"Stop it—we're going to focus now on why exactly Sal is—why you are still here."

"It's six-thirty, no?"

"Don't play dumb," she said, her neck vein strumming itself clean. "I'm talking about Seven Corners."

"Adie's the one who's leaving. Sal's keeping the house."

"Salvador, I'm talking to *you*." Even though she said my name—my full name, like a mother, and yes, it gave me chills—I couldn't intuit who her words were for. "Don't you know that there's something powerful in the act of leaving? I mean it. Leaving makes it so that all you come across is something you've found." She stood up and paced the room, like she was dictating a future speech. "And really, a sense of self is only everything that a person finds and decides to keep. I want you to find some things for yourself. Do you hear me? Salvador, is there anything here to find?"

I thought about the dirty house, the empty theater. I mentally flipped the pages of the Denny's menu. I had not found a single dish that didn't ultimately make me sick. But hadn't I found Carla?

"Wait," I said. "Are you breaking up with me?"

She sat down. "The fact that you'd even use that language proves my decision to—"

"To leave."

"To move and reduce the size of my practice."

"To abandon us," I said, squeezing the Matchbox car in my hand until its little plastic windshield snapped. I couldn't feel my breath in my mouth, and I told Carla this. I may have shouted it.

"You're sick, Sal. What are you all doing there at the diner? Besides making yourselves sicker?"

"Belonging."

"You need something better to bond you to the world, something more than your fucking therapist. You need an identity, and probably a strong prescription."

"I don't know," I said, down on the carpet. "I just don't know."

"Yes, you do."

For all the feelings I still have—I am thankful for how long she let me lie there on the floor.

"You know it's illegal what she's doing," Jed said the first week of the transition. Carla started seeing her remaining clients in her home, at least until the place sold. "That block's not zoned for private business."

"I have something to bring to the table," Jones said, before explaining that his sister, an officer with Seven Corners PD with whom Jones had been crashing, shared with him reports of excessive loitering on Carla's street. His sister had heard him rave about Carla, and she wanted to make sure he wasn't doing anything stupid. "So, I'm asking you all," Jones said. "Has anyone been doing anything stupid?"

Jed began to cry into his big red napkin, and my breath came back. Luckily it didn't have to come to a restraining order—Jed agreed he would leave. He'd been leaving things in her mailbox daily, little things like notes and stones and pieces of trees, things he had noticed and wanted to show her. We dealt with the issue internally, as we did the night Thin Bill shared Carla's phone number. A month later we helped Jed with his move, waved bye as he cried in the cab of his little Ford Ranger, belongings spilling from that overfull truck bed.

They would never know it had been me pacing up and down the

opposite side of Carla's street. I never crossed closer than the yellow line. What troubles me the most is that, at the time, I didn't even see that man as me. The creep out there in the Steelers jacket—that was Sal.

Without her, Jones actually got better—a little stuffed up on downers, but it helped him out of his hole. He found a counselor in York City, progressed to monthly, then four times a year, and now I have a letter from him I don't like to think about, full of praise for a cliché, bearded God. I found Orrin on Facebook, but he never posts. Every picture shows him with a smile that I hate myself for reading as fake. I notice that he now has braces. Carla always said that progress takes all shapes.

In the end, it was Carla who left. It seemed powerful to me, but I hope it didn't feel like fleeing. Which makes me wonder how many times, for her, a move has been a necessity, an escape from the need of men. Men like us. Men like me, clinging to the power line despite the death of the tree. I hope like hell the truth is that she simply needed to find a place, for herself, where things could still be found.

Now she practices ten towns down Lincoln Highway, where her new rates are mean, and my newest job's plan won't cover things like Carla. Necessary things. Sublime things. Preexisting. I heard the high school closed the art wing and laid off two counselors in the same summer. I heard the banks fucked us, they're going bankrupt. I've heard that if you look at America from above, say from a plane, there's no denying it's riddled with cracks. Flawed geography. The foundation—spiderwebbed. If I'm ever up in the air I will look to confirm this. What I can say is I feel a shudder beneath my car tires, like I'm vibrating against a track, desperate for a power station to send me into the next corner, but there's nothing on the horizon. Even as the car putters to a stop—

—everything built shakes.

Tonight my kitchen shift is dead, so I walk sluggish laps through the dining room—if I find a tear in a booth seat's upholstery, I'll stitch it up. Tight, with matching thread, though the fix rarely holds more than a couple days. I refer to my work as my practice, and somehow this helps.

I regret that I wrote down her home number, the one Thin Bill read off to us that night in that corner booth, now empty. When I get real low I type those ten numbers into my phone, even though I know the chance is slim it's still hers after all these years. Just the act of typing it, button by button, is enough. Though I'll admit I sometimes do press *Call*. But I always—and if this isn't progress—hit *End* before the zeroes appear.

BLACK SANDS

"If it's ever love," Dad says about Nurse Toni, "I think we'll know it."

But we've been outside in a tornado and didn't even know it. Two summers back, biking along Lake Michigan. It was impossible to pedal. All of Portage was a mess. Beside us, gulls beat their wings but went nowhere. Dad kept saying, "One heck of a storm we're in." We got off and trudged with our bikes at an angle so that the wind couldn't put us into the drink. The rain fell in white whips, like a cartoon. I kept asking, "Is this a tornado? Dad, are we in a tornado?" The sky was practically green. "I think if we were in a tornado," he said, "we wouldn't need to ask." I could almost make out our apartment building through the dark of the storm when a big gust took my bike into the Little Calumet River. We just watched it swirling in the water. Then Dad pushed his in.

And we ran.

But Dad's in love.

"Only with you, Sabrina," he says, singing out the last vowel in my name. His girlfriend, Nurse Toni, will be over soon, and he's got the unchipped plates on the table and The Boss on the stereo.

"Seems like a production," I say. He looks at me like he doesn't know who I am and straightens his fat '80s tie down over the sauce spot on his button-up. Tonight he's half Bible salesman, half Mr.

Feeny, half woolly mammoth. He shampooed his hair so it's all poofy and airy, bunched up around his ears in thick, gray-sand curls.

"What production?" he says. "We're just hosting dinner." I hold back from telling him he has a thread. It hangs from his shirttail like a leash. He's in love. But so am I. Miguel will be here any minute.

"I'm getting food out tonight," I say.

"Sab." He sighs. "We knew about this dinner, this night. This isn't news."

He's going to propose to her. I can feel it. All week the apartment's had a third heartbeat, something heavy and pulsing living with us—a ring. A diamond in a black, snapped-shut box.

"I know, Dad, but I'll be home then, and we'll play Scrabble or something." He follows me to the edge of the kitchen tile but won't come any further, one of his classic adages being: *Never leave the kitchen or you'll forget about the food.* The sauce spurts onto the stove.

"So you're gonna leave me for Arby's?" he says, adding one of my old eye-rolls.

"Mhm."

"With Miguel."

"Correct." I try to never lie to him, my first best friend.

"You're fourteen," he says. "We're not in love here, you know that right?"

With him I am always *we*, he is always *we*, and anything he cares about sticks to the orbit of *us*. Behind him, I can see my final report card for June—all Bs, comments like *Often unprepared*, *Pleasure to have in class*, and *Struggles with focus*. He doesn't take his eyes off me.

"Correct. Miguel and me are not," I say. "But you are. Admit it."

Their fling started in coffee shops two years ago, after we moved Mom from the hospital to that assisted living facility out in Hobart which I call The Brick (the whole red building looks like one ungodly dropped brick. Even my grandparents, who live nearby and visit Mom almost daily, call it The Brick). For months, the story went: Dad was helping the nurse write a memoir. Dinner every Wednesday—memoir. Hikes on Saturdays—memoir. Her name written on his hand like a fifth grader, reminding him to reread the newest chapter of—her freaking memoir. Dad went to technical school to learn a trade called *tool and die*. He worked at US Steel (where he met Mom) for almost thirty years and then, for the last three, at Payless in the dying mall. What I'm saying is there are no books in our apartment besides my mother's journal.

He and Toni pronounce it *memwah*.

Dad still claims the steel plant laid him off, but I think he quit. Reminded him too much of Mom—all that raw plastic, plans, molds. This was three years ago, after she started losing it (forgetting which lever made the car move, what a storm was, where we lived) and stopped working.

The door buzzes, and I let her up. Dad turns back to the elements of his dinner, the trappings of his night. He slices a bread loaf with vigor and inaccuracy. A quick double-knock and Nurse Toni comes through the door. She's wearing a color of blue I have never seen before. I forget to say hello.

"Evening, love," she says. "You know Miguel's double-parked?" Dad saws the bread end and it falls to the floor. There's no dog to come grab it up. We all just look at it. "I love you, Dad," I say, pulling on a sweatshirt, leaving. He doesn't come to the door for a hug, stays planted in the kitchen. His smile is huge, goofy, and he's sweating. For some reason, I don't know, I feel like this is the last time I'll ever see him. He looks so young. I order myself: *Remember his face.*

✳

Back in those early Nurse Toni days, when her memoir was a shabby half draft, we were at Outback Steakhouse and I'd just brattily asked the waitress, "Honey, could hook us up with more rolls?" Dad asked me to tell Toni some life lessons he'd taught me. I did not explain the sweet-talking power he'd gained from being a salesman, how I'd been trying to hone this skill myself, because even though I'm short, thin, weak, often fearful of forgetting something, I know there is power in how people respond to what you say. Instead, I answered, "We should always be in this together." They both squinted. She smiled. I told her about the bikes in the river during the tornado, which had happened earlier that summer. I didn't mean for the story to end where it did, with us coming home to find Cumin, our family's black Lab, missing. But it's what I remembered. Such a happy dog, pant like a smile. A new basket of rolls came, and the waiter winked. Cumin was Mom's dog. Heat rose off the bread like fog. I had taught her the two-handed high-five and how to play dead. I didn't look at anyone and stopped talking. We put up posters. We were all looking at the bread. I didn't want any.

Because he holds down a job and has never been in an accident, Dad trusts Miguel. Which is more than I can say for myself. I mean: He's cute. Tall. Sweet. Works at Arby's. I like to measure, photograph, and compare to earlier dates his little mustache. Hearing him talk about his summer trips to Guatemala, I feel *there*. I swear I know the volcanoes. I'm taking Spanish 2 in the fall. He never flexes his arms on purpose. But, I have seen him rip his passenger door handle off after the movie *Signs* made him cry (I'd seen his tears in the parking lot and giggled). I kept the door handle as a souvenir. A reminder, an omen. We've been dating since December.

The June night is a low bluish-purple. My boyfriend's car is red.

My door doesn't work now, so he can't get out and open it for me like he did on our first few dates, very gentlemanly. Instead, he turns his music down and reaches across the passenger seat to open my door. He strains when he does this, gets a sick look on his face as he opens and then pushes with the tips of his fingers. The door bounces open only an inch, but I catch it. Inside, I kiss his cheek.

"Hola, baby," I say. "Take me to the curly fries."

And he does.

Last winter, Dad made Miguel drive him around for half an hour. I stood in the living room, watched from the window as it started to snow. Later, he said Miguel had a good handshake and spoke *surprisingly fluent English.*

"Well he's second generation so, yeah."

"You know what I mean," he said. Dad doesn't try to be racist, but he does hit the power locks the second we enter Gary. He's okay with me seeing Miguel as long as I don't call it love. Nurse Toni is nice and sometimes gorgeous and a great sport in board games, and I just want them to call it love. Dad's afraid I'm going to get dramatic, claim his love's been allocated to someone else, have to live with a heart half-full or something. "I'm practically fifteen," I'll remind him. "Grow up."

One additional thing I love about Dad: he doesn't understand irony. Which probably contributed to Mom's plan to leave him. Divorce was her idea, floated long before the early days of her hospitalization. An idea she'd had in her head for years, even before me, I bet. When the diagnosis came, she demanded it. Dad said he was shocked but didn't want to fight with someone in a hospital. I know it was a long time coming. Read it in her diary when I was ten and the library was flooded and I was devouring every book in my mother's room. I remember it like lyrics: *I don't know if I can make it until Sab's in college.*

Some days I think THIS IS THE DAY. Dreams of packing her in the car
and gunning it down I-80 West, south all the way to Mexico. But I know
if I left, I'd leave them both. Something feels crooked in my head. I could
go tomorrow. But I can wait. There's time. There's too much.

They're out of curly fries at Miguel's Arby's, the one in east Gary, so we veer out of the drive-thru, park, and he goes in to chew out the nightshift punks. When he comes back, I say, "Looks like we're going to East Chicago." Miguel sighs, turns the ignition. But before we move backward, he reaches into the bookbag he keeps between his legs while driving, and puts his other hand on my thigh.

"I want to tell you something," he says.

"Want to tell me why you wouldn't let me go with you into Arby's?"

"Huh? No."

"Well, why couldn't I come in?" I've already forgotten that he has something to tell me.

"Don't want you to see me like that," he says.

"Like what?" I want to hear him say it. He sighs, puts both hands back on the wheel. We leave. I roll my window down so my hair snaps around like propellers.

I ask him again at a red light. He never takes his eyes off the road, even at lights. It is rare that he looks at me directly, but he's always listening. "Like what?" I repeat. The light goes green but his car doesn't move. He's looking at me. "Like a madman?"

The cars behind us honk. Miguel bites his bottom lip and narrows his eyes at me. "Forget it, Sabrina," is all he says, his hard arms tense. The night is quiet, radio off. We roll forward, and the argument passes. While he pursues our food, I relax and recite my stories.

I knew Miguel was necessary for my life when I first told him about my mom, about the early onset Alzheimer's and her bike accident, and how Dad wouldn't let me talk about this stuff because he kept saying we needed to be somewhere, or we needed sleep, or we needed to be really brave. Miguel set down his cup, wiped the drips of milkshake from his mustache, and reached his hand across the center console. I hadn't even started crying yet.

His cold hand on my bare knee, he said, "You don't have to be brave with me."

That happened four months ago, and I haven't stopped talking since. As soon as he picks me up I say everything Dad doesn't want to hear. My dread. All of my Big Life Things that Mom will miss. Like the face Dad made when I told him about my period. Or my guilt for being so selfish. My suspicions about what the other patients (sorry, *residents*) at The Brick say and do to her, their youngest, prettiest, most sarcastic inmate (sorry, *neighbor*). My fears about losing my memory like Mom.

Miguel listens to everything. And we drive. Or eat fries, slurp shakes, sit in the sand at Dunes National Park, watch Lake Michigan simmer. Mainly, I tell him story after story. Memories with Dad. Memories of Mom that I can't corroborate because, whenever Miguel gets me to agree to visit her, she won't even say my name. I fill in parts with imagination. They're my stories anyway.

"You have to remember this," I tell him, "in case some day I can't."

I want reassurance, a double, a second chance, a backup brain.

And all Miguel wants is to listen, and to eventually take my virginity in this Civic.

Mom and Dad met at US Steel, at the snack machines. One day, Mom bought two sodas, took one, and walked away. Her hair was chopped short like mine, alluring, way before it was cool.

Dad was all, "You forgot this." And she was like, "It's on me."

"Which soda?" Miguel asks every time I tell this one. So detail-driven, really listening. You have to love that.

"Dr Pepper."

"Ahh," he says, like it makes complete sense. Like he can taste it.

Next day, Dad, with his mullet and everything, said dinner was on him. They stayed late eating these hamburgers that fell frozen out of the machine and you cooked them in the microwave. That first night they started talking about the future, what they wanted from life, drawing a blueprint.

"Just goes to show," I explain to Miguel, taking a sip of my watery soda. "Puppy love is a real thing. It lasts different lengths of time for everyone." My parents were wed as puppies. Jeb, my brother, showed up within a year. Me, not for twelve and a half more years, but that's another story.

Miguel goes: "You and me been together over half a year. Feels like forever."

"Puppies," I insist.

"Nah," he says, turning left, his right hand on my thigh. "We got a jaguar love."

Nurse Toni was good to my mother. Best nurse we had before moving her to The Brick. Always with little gifts. Spending downtime and shift breaks in Mom's room. She'd sit in this brown folding chair, scribbling down notes, the fragments of her *memwah*, listening to my mother talk about nothing. She would make all the proper noises, the *Mhm*s, the *I see*s, the *Isn't that just the truth*s.

I don't like to look at Nurse Toni, but I'd like to be able to sit on the other side of a confessional from her, explain my theory about Mom's disease, about how, if I have it too (which, the chances for early onset Alzheimer's being passed from mother to daughter are, well . . . I haven't looked it up, okay? I just don't want to know yet), then the whole timeline of my life is different. My life is actually shortened by a third. So, in order to experience life fairly, I have to move up all of the important dates by 33 percent. Traveling the world in love and having sex at fourteen makes sense, because people with eighty-five-to-ninety-year-long lives would do it in their twenties or thirties. This is my only life.

I tried to give Toni a compliment once. We were en route to a party in Ogden Dunes and for some weird reason both me and Toni sat in the back seat. We laughed about it at first, but then no one got out. We called Dad *boy* and said things like *The Dunes, boy. And make it snappy!* It was funny. I wanted to compliment her on her style. She looked like warm rain. I went for it, but all I got was *warm*. She didn't say thank you. She got out on my side, and when she slid across the seat our arms touched, and I can tell you this: She was. Warm.

At the next Arby's we order three large fries and a massive Dr Pepper. Miguel pays, parks, and turns to me. He opens his mouth, but then he closes it. A school of crotch rockets screams past, wheelieing.

Over a decade into the problem of their marriage, my parents made me by accident. Camping. It was a last Hail Mary to save the life they hated. And who doesn't hate camping? The whole idea. It's like when a new collectibles store opens inside Dad's dying mall—no one wants this, everything is old, it's not even fun to look at, so why bother? Apparently, it was muggy hot. Bug bites polka-dotted Mom's face. The campground hosted an exhibit on turkey vultures during which the de-taloned show bird got loose and bit the ranger's arm, hit a vein, blood went everywhere.

"Is this a truthful story?" Miguel asks.

My parents retreated to the campsite and never made a fire but just went straight to bed with a six-pack and drank them laying down, which can screw you up, I guess. In the middle of the night, all sweaty and tipsy and atop rocks and probably lousy with Lyme—they jumped each other's bones. Ta-da! Mom was forty-two.

Miguel moves his seat back as far as it will go and gives me those eyes.

As if my parents are what I want at the front of my brain when I lose it.

The Arby's lot fills with suped-up Volkswagens. "Time to go back to Portage," I say.

"For privacy?" Miguel says.

"No, because that's where home is," I say with a little laugh.

"Whatever you want," he sighs. Miguel is the son of "illegal immigrants." But he's a citizen. Thank you, DREAM Act. I call my boyfriend a Dream-Actor, because sometimes he seems unreal. Like how even during dreams of my mom—she's driving me out west to start college, we're chain-chewing packs of gum, the sun is pink, and after I'm settled in my dorm she keeps on south to Mexico—I can realize, within the dream, that something's off. It's too good to be true.

So, sometimes I worry about Miguel, whether his feelings for me are too good to be true. Maybe all he really wants from me is something I'm not ready to want back.

With what's left of our fries, we drive back to my flat rectangle of a town and he steers into Imagination Glen Park. We sit on the bleachers, watching ballers play Around the World under lights. Everyone is missing. Miguel wants to know what I'm doing this summer and have I ever been on a plane? He reaches into his pocket and says, "What color is sand?"

I can see some in the distance, past the soccer field. I eat a curly fry dipped in hot sauce. "Beige," I say, "like the universe."

He hands me a ticket and a passport application.

"Sand is black," he whispers. With him this close to me, it's confirmed: his mustache has gotten longer. It turns out this ticket to Guatemala is his, but he can get one for me (and he'll pay for it) if we act soon. That's how he says it. "We have to act soon."

My memories of life with Mom as a little kid aren't bad, but they never feel warm. Sometimes when Dad's drunk he gossips sadly, saying Mom was detached, distant, spotty with sympathy—the I-STEP vocab word would be *aloof*. All of which could have been due to her hating her marriage and feeling generally disillusioned with her mid-life. I see kids at the park with their moms and they so often look like friends.

The thing I realize now is that I was just a big-ass brat. The kind of fit I could throw in public, at the drop of a hat, you should have seen it. It was beyond screaming, kicking, hair sticking to my teary cheeks—I once shoved over a sunglasses rack. If Mom let go of my hand, there's no telling what would be ruined. Mannequins, disrobed. Mall fountains were pools, toilets.

Once afternoon we'd left the zoo early because the dolphin exhibit was closed and I'd tried to break the octopus tank with my little fists. Mom lectured me in the traffic leaving Chicago. She wouldn't stop. I began to scream. I was seven. I didn't stop. Our A/C wasn't working.

She grabbed me by the face, squeezing my cheeks with her right hand like a fruit. She yelled, "I will slap your fucking face off your fucking head!"

I stopped crying. I shut up. I smiled. She laughed. We both laughed so hard. I was laughing more at her laugh than at anything.

The cars behind us would not lay off their horns. I leaned my head out the window and repeated her words to the world in a roar, and I created a silence.

It sounds like anger, or the quiet rustling of frustration, whenever I move Miguel's hand out of my lap. He grumbles but passes it off like he's clearing his clogged throat. The kissing part of the night always goes like this. The incremental movement of his hand up my leg, like rolling over onto the TV remote, volume turning up one notch—11 to 12—every few seconds—12 to 13—until it's screaming loud—28 29 30—and it's waking both your parents in their separate rooms, and the dog, and the dog next door, and you have no idea where the remote even is anymore so you just unplug the TV. Miguel exhales slowly like my mouth is a cigarette. Eyes squinted and glassy. He has my hand. I wonder if he will rip it off or place it in his lap. He does neither. What he does is not let me talk the whole drive home. He finds the station I don't like (107.7 HOT Country) and blasts it. No kiss goodnight. None of the standard apologies (*Sabrina, I was carrying away . . .*), not even a look.

When I unlatch my seatbelt all he says is, "Guate."

I know if I go it will be the greatest trip of my life, and I will become a woman.

And I know that Mom will have no memory, no say, no hand in any of it. For her, the trip will have never happened, and the way I am changed by it will never be discernible. I could come home, tanned and taller and talkative, but my stories will be nothing more than her little forgettable dreams.

It is ten o'clock. Miguel, always on time. I won't get out of the car. Dad's watching from the window of our third-floor walk-up, waving, just starting to worry. But I need to go someplace else. Miguel refuses.

He reaches across my personal space and cracks the door for me.

"Take me," I say, grabbing his hand and pressing it to my chest, "to The Brick."

I should've known that Dad would chase me, but I wasn't thinking about him anymore.

It happened on a bike ride.

Mom's top hobby was riding the paved Portage trails. They're luxurious, wide, smooth, and wind through wooded paths, over railroad tracks, bringing you all the way to the beach, the dunes, the now federally protected shoreline park US Steel built to give back to the community they had nearly destroyed with toxic runoff. Mom and Dad used to take walks along those trails when she was pregnant with my brother. They'd get off work and walk right across the parking lot to the beach.

What I mean is my mother knew the trails well. But one day (I was eleven, at home, in my room, reading) she veered from the park path, jumped the curb, bounced across the grass median and into Route 12 traffic. Luckily, she was only clipped by the fat side mirror of an F-350—but she went down hard. The Trek crunched beneath the tires of a semi, and her right arm snapped. The ulna jutted out her skin, split into the point of a spear. She didn't cry. She'd forgotten how, I think.

Soon she forgot a lot of things, mostly about how time worked. The doctors called it shock. Nurse Toni called it normal. For weeks they called it that. She'd get a phrase trapped in her head and it became the only thing she could say for hours. A snag can be anything, but it's usually a piece of language (*Bike chain needs grease*, or *War—what is it good for?*) that falls like a boulder between the sides of her brain. One of the creepier mantras was: *The mouth bone's connected to the—head bone.* Finally an older, sharper-dressed doctor saw her and called it Alzheimer's. Mom was fifty-three.

After getting out of the hospital, US Steel took her off the floor, put her in an office. Simple tasks. Emails. Filing. But she'd cc the whole office pitches for pyramid schemes. She'd search things on the internet even I don't have the courage to search. Dildos. Coffins.

"I know you've heard all this before," I say to Miguel at the final red light. "I'm sorry."

"You get better at telling it."

"You just mean each time it's shorter."

"No, you get more . . . you get more to the heart of it?" He's using a phrase my mother used when she told me the tent story, my conception story. *We went out into the woods to get to the heart of it.* I'd almost forgotten that part.

Miguel, sometimes I wanted to jump your bones.

I know which door the tattooed cafeteria guys smoke outside of, and it's always unlocked. Miguel waits in the car. The wind's picking up. The cottonwood trees are sailing their stuffing through the air of the parking lot like a snow globe.

I climb the stairs until Lake Michigan's shining in the window and dodge two texting orderlies. Mom normally bounces between phases of sleeping forever and worrisome insomnia. Tonight, my hope is for insomnia. I haven't been here in over a month, because I'm a monster.

The room's only light is a full moon and the glaring red eye of her corner TV on standby. I pause by her bathroom door. The mementos of her past—the family photos, maps of Mexico, the witty T-shirts too big for her now—they fill the walls with color. In this way, her room looks a lot like mine.

"Announce yourself," she says to the dark room.

"It is I, Sabrina."

"The teenaged witch?"

I cross over to the window. My name was Dad's idea. The air conditioning freezes me to the sill. Mom doesn't like hugs, kisses, intimacy. She's worried about the passage of SARS or something. Her mouth is in fact covered with a pale pink doctor's mask. She looks so young. She is. Fifty-six.

At her bedside now, I get the courage for eye contact—she seems lucid. "Have you ever been to Guatemala?" I ask.

"When I make a joke, can you please laugh? The doctor says—"

"It's the best medicine?"

"Social lubricant. It's supposed to make me seem—"

"Mom, I was joking." She laughs, mechanically, kind of Vader-like behind her mask, which makes me laugh. I don't know why I've been avoiding her. We're laughing. We have something. But then I move to flick the light switch and she scolds me. She wants it dark.

"Why would a twelve-year-old girl need to go to Guatemala?"

"A boy," I say, ignoring her error. "Bridges, birds, lose my virginity, black sand beaches."

She pulls off her mask to show me her tight, disapproving frown. So I explain to her my Alzheimer's math. How I'm in such a hurry to get it all in before things begin to disappear. The room is quiet, my fantasies and theories just hanging there. I decide to turn on the light.

"Sabrina, I'm sorry I left." Mom closes her eyes. "You know how much I love you?"

"You didn't love *us*," I whisper, speaking for Dad too. I know he and Nurse Toni are searching Portage for me right now—that's love. "I read every page of your journal before you moved out."

"I did not keep a journal. But if I did, then you'd know I love you and only wanted you to be free of all this sickness. I knew this was coming before anyone, before the car crash."

"Bike accident," I say. "But Mom, you can't protect me from it. If I have it, I have it."

"You don't have it."

"If I do, then isn't it better to learn from you how to handle it?"

Mom squints her eyes tight and fans her hands up and down. She's saying: *Look, this is it. This is your lesson.* Her dinner sits on a tray untouched. A car horn blares down below.

"You won't believe it when I tell you, Sabrina. Forgetting is the most relieving feeling. Our brains love us. They do us so many favors."

"Why would you want to forget?"

"Memories weigh us down," she says. "I feel so light I could float to the ceiling." I watch to see if she does. "Do you love Michael?" she asks.

"Miguel, and don't change the sub—"

"Love is illegal," Mom says. "Don't get fucking caught with it." There's a little band of moonlight on the floor. I move from the window to stand in it, so my mother can see my face.

"It's just puppy love, right?" I say.

"The dog just, just . . . just got away." I don't even have to look at her glazy eyes above that mask to know she's caught on a snag. *The dog just got away,* she says again. And again. They say that when Mom gets caught the right move is to redirect with questions and prompts, like a teacher.

"You remember Cumin?" I say, moving toward her cold dinner.

"Dog just got away."

That fast I give up. In defeat, I grab a dinner roll from the tray and rip it in half.

"Dog just got away." She accepts her half of bread and sinks into her floral sheets.

"Away," I say, moving toward the door, leaving without answers, with only a feeling, a new little fragment of a story to tell Miguel and hide from Dad. I might change the end though. Tell it so that I held her hand until she fell asleep, that I quietly read aloud from her journal.

Away, away, I can hear it from the lobby. The orderlies want to know what I think I'm doing here at eleven at night. "I don't remember," I say, admitting my biggest fear. I already forget what really happened. I take the stairs slowly, one at a time. *Away, away, away.*

Miguel's mad. I want him to ask me about her, how she's doing, how I feel—but he's silent. Eyes closed. The car's off. The cotton is stacking up on his windshield like a blanket. How long was I gone?

"We can go," I say. He's a statue. I grab the last cold curly fry. "Darling, spirit us away into the night!"

"You want to go home now." He doesn't say it like a question. "You have no more use for me anymore tonight." This sounds like every time Dad lectures me: a man, still as ice, speaking in quiet, uninflected statements, each beginning with that awful word *You.* And I don't speak. I recite to myself my best memories. Cumin running through the park with every other dog in pursuit. My brother's graduation from basic training and the four of us—me, Mom, Dad, and all the way up on the little white stage, Jeb—all crying. Each for different reasons. Miguel's glance at the drive-thru, looking right past Dad, right at me. Coloring monsoons all over Mom's cast.

"Are you listening?" Miguel says.

"I left something inside."

"You aren't listening to my words," he says. "I don't feel any love from you."

I reach for my door handle. Miguel hits the power locks and grabs my arm.

"But I left my . . . " I can't think of a lie. I keep trying to open the door. "Please let me—" He grips me harder. For the first time, I feel his bare power. "Let go!"

"Look at me!" Miguel yells. "You left me down here an hour, meanwhile your dad probably has the cops looking for his only daughter. If he ever lets me near you again it will be a miracle. Or no—it will be more of me running your errands. I want to take you to an adventure. I want to teach you about my life, get you out of sickness. You say nothing. You never ask me any single questions. You look out windows. You talk. I kiss you, your mouth dries up."

Turning from his rage, I look out the window and, Jesus, Toni's staring back. She can't find the handle and smacks the glass. On Miguel's side is my father, pulling at the locked door. His tie flies in the wind. Miguel drops my arm. I sink low in the seat, trying to hide. Dad's yelling is furious but muffled, like a storm one town over. Toni's fists pound my window. A diamond shines on her finger. The ring doesn't fit, so it spins as she punches, falls to the front of her finger, scratches little notes in the glass. I wonder if she'll put this moment in her memoir. If she'll use my real name.

"Sabrina!" Dad calls.

"We're in love!" I scream back through the window, as we enter the eye of it.

All I remember of that fight now is quiet. Maybe that's what shock is. Maybe I never felt so close to both parents.

Because I was selfish. I still am. I was allowed to be. Goddamn it, I still am. Believe me when I say I know it, when I say, *Don't make me tell this all again.* Don't remind me of the first love I lost that night. How the bruise on my arm looked like the state of Indiana, and I cried when it faded. Please, just don't. *We never leave the kitchen, or we'll forget about the food.* Don't remind me of the dog that barked as Miguel's tires peeled off to the east. Or Mom at her third-story window, watching down on us, praying for the end of memory. Don't remind me of that night outside The Brick, the cotton swirling around us like a snowstorm, where, out of spite, I told Dad we did it, how I lied, proud, about Miguel and I having sex. How I never let him call me *us* again. How in the parking lot, Miguel gone, my father and I screaming, Toni pushed between us. How gently she held back my fists. And later, in the back seat, exhausted and nodding off against her warm shoulder, I said the ring looked nice and meant it.

K.

1. On that Fishtown roof we laid down cardboard from the Papa John's dumpster and danced. Two b-boys, but you were better. The sun had just set, the sky all about that smoky purple light. I set the camcorder on the A/C unit and framed you. Thumbs up. Your shirt off. Your face never not ready to be legendary, Wheaties box, movie poster. Elbows loose. Gravel shifting beneath the cardboard, so on six-steps it looked like we were skating, floating, still but still moving. We didn't even play a song, I just clapped, because Fuck it, we'd add the track later when something worthy dropped, the new Nas, who knows. This tape, your ticket, my street cred, that bandwagon, or at the very least our guarantee readymade nostalgia like Holy shit—Oh my god when we'd find the film decades later in a box after moving to the suburbs, our kids saying, "Daddy, what *is*?" What did we do? We were teenaged, but we knew the tape was the thing, to have proof, to hold in your hands what you'd made. To be named. Like those all-city writers who bombed the maroon SEPTA trolley tour, foreigners gawking at all the thousand city murals like, Bitch you got one right out the window, just look at where your hand's hanging, haha. We could see them from the roof. We had a laugh. It was fun. It was more than that, breaking. It was . . . what'd you always say about dance?

2. Then that night manager wanted us off the roof. We yelled down some dumb shit like we were allowed, legit. He sold pizzas. He had

pimples. He—I can only see this now—was a kid just doing his job. But we hated his tone, his acne scars. We talked back in kicks, freezes, downrock, windmill, suicide, tossing our arms around like dirty jokes. And when the police showed, you grabbed the camera, needed just one lone frame of their red and blue lights blinking. A perfect resolution to our tape's story. Remember your mantra, that white tee you sharpied with softy letters? EVERY STORY IS A DANCE WITH NO BEGINNING. We were gonna sell that design. But the cop called us down. He said, "Now."

3. And he didn't help us. No, just called for backup and watched our asses climbing backwards down the gutter. When I touched the ground, I sprinted deep into the alley, but then he cornered you at the dumpster, threw you to the blacktop. Broken glass in your braids—remember later how I tried to pick it out, but you slapped my hand away? We walked home over sidewalks in silence. You had the slightest limp. I didn't bring it up. I said Peace. You never said Peace.

4. My daughters asked me why I used to breakdance, which (thank God) is an easier one than *Why don't you still?* I remember I broke to stay sober, needed an addiction different from my dad's, but you, K, you danced for transportation. *Easiest way to leave a place is out the mind.* I remember you broke with your eyes closed. We put our energies into these tapes, these moves, crimes but victimless. We could b-boy anyplace—only climbed that roof for the view. As if anybody watching the tape would be able to look past you.

5. That night, the door to your aunt's building. You turned to me and made a face. You turned it inside out.

✳

6. Our tape scared my girls. "Daddy's on a roof?" They'd seen a neighbor fall from one. Sits crooked in a wheelchair under the carport now. They giggle at him from our front yard but pray for him in church. You never did have the leg looked at, never watched the video either. Even though I called your aunt's house on the daily, asking you to come over, let's play the tape, and I had this application Mrs. Raines wanted me to give you for UArts, but you swore: *They don't wanna let us dance there. They wanna choreograph us.* You always sounded right. But that was the problem, most times it was only the sound.

7. My girls, tonight, on the back patio—they're trying to be you. I'm grading papers. Kia's tucked in a ball on the concrete, and Becca's turning her in circles. Backspin. You knew that move. You still know that move. It's the last one on the tape before the sirens. I know that cop said shit to you, whispered in your ear, bent your arms back like an airflare, kicked your knee. You didn't do anything. I didn't do anything, standing back a hundred feet. We hadn't done anything. They didn't know what we were doing. We knew what we were doing. They kept looking around at the ground for dice. Motherfucking dice? A one hitter, baggies. Roaches. What's it matter? Then he looked right at your body. Stared at your sweat. Like a shirt the way it covered you. You did nothing. The sun's gone tonight. We're out of light.

8. And what have you done with yourself, with life, your body, the way it can move, freeze, break? With me. I found you online, your name listed in a short article. With mug shots. They got you. With a shotgun. Regardless of whoever did whatever it was. With the tape, in my old notebook, I found your email—bboykk@aim.com—but it bounced back. With gibberish. Now I'm writing on yellow paper. With a pen. Like the way I wrote my rhymes, because my moves were

weak I thought maybe I could rap. With fire. But you were right when you said I couldn't go even eight bars without lying. Like I did just now: 'cus I don't know if you did what's in the paper. They frame you? Maybe. I don't know anything. Another lie: I don't know if you did shit with your life or not, 'cus I left, stopped visiting, and you used to call me at my job, after my night classes, the phone blinking red beside the register out at that West Chester Wawa, your dumb drunk crank calls, how I always hung up. With violence.

9. Kia asks why Mommy's the only one with friends. I gotta chat politics and basketball with their husbands. I don't know the rules to basketball. What color's a fucking basketball? One time back in college, when she was just my girl, she asked me to list all the people I'd kissed. I laughed, I don't know. "You seem upset," she said.

10. All that mattered was letting it go. But Mrs. Raines—remember her History class?—she knew too. Said all that matters is being true.

11. Remember picking our b-boy names from a thesaurus? Sharpies on our arms, you did mine, I did yours. I remember cutting the sleeves off your orange windbreaker. Trendsetter. Vanguard. I've never seen another body move like yours. Did we call that night manager *faggot*? We were laughing, but did I threaten his life? Did he ask what we were doing on the roof? Was he just curious? Why were we afraid? Was it for no reason? Why did you stay? Some kind of statement nobody could decode? Did that squad car follow us home? Did it follow you alone?

12. My wife owns every season of *So You Think You Can Dance* on DVD. Calls it comfort food. I did a shitty 2000 at our wedding,

turning on my hands like a top. She pop-locked. I wish you'd been there. Ripped a tear right through my jacket. Fucking breaking in a tux. You believe this? You were the better dancer. But you needed me next to you for proof. Beside me you shined. Your fingers were callused but still soft as communion bread. I'm drunk off wine. In the motherfucking suburbs. And almost out of paper.

—B

Fuck.

I was gonna leave it at a twelve-bar, let the beat rock through the last four, but I forgot about the video, the whole reason I'm writing . . .

. . . forget your sweaty braids whipping like branches in a storm, white kicks scuffed gray and brown, the fact that the camera wasn't even focused on us, or ours. Think only of your two legs and an arm held stiff in the air, making the shape of your first initial—K. I made this four-second clip, K. If we'd had more time, K, if the cop call hadn't gotten through, if the pimpled kid wasn't scared, K, if police couldn't speed, if I hadn't run away, K, you would keep dancing through every letter. Until the whole city knew your name. It plays over and over on my desktop. The girls clap every time it's done. K. They're never not clapping for you, for you to finish the sentence.

COWBOY MAN, MAJOR PLAYER

I'm not sure who I am, but I know who I've been.
—MODEST MOUSE, "Make Everyone Happy/Mechanical Birds"

Cowboy Dan finds himself in a meme.

Summer is over and he's on a Dell at the Texarkana Public Library, researching two things: a new place to live, and bass tabs for a song he heard on the radio, a song about crashing your car into the bridge, watching it burn, and not giving a shit. In the comment section of Ultimateguitartabs.com, he sees a square photograph of himself on stage at the Reservation, bass listing left on his hip, right leg atop the monitor in a power stance. The photographer caught him mid-wink, with one eye clamped shut and the other fluttering, like the lead-up to a sneeze, but that's not the embarrassing part. The embarrassing part is that he's giving a big thumbs-up, and his thumb is plugging the mouth of a Lone Star beer bottle. The beer slides down his arm, drips from his elbow, and puddles on the monitor. Heavy white text captions the image, half of it ("COWBOY MAN'S A") placed above his Stetson, the other half ("MAJOR PLAYER") lining the bottom. He stands at the computer, staring at a photo he does not remember being taken. That club closed in 2011—isn't it a clinic now? And that band broke up years ago.

"Excuse me, sir," says a nosy man with a name badge. Cowboy Dan flinches, leans forward to block the image from view. "Computers are for research, not for making memes."

"Something feels wrong about this," Garrett says and turns off the microphone.

"Shaker's too loud," says Gina, dropping her sticks. "I've been saying it over and over."

Cowboy Dan sets the shaker, large as an ostrich egg, on the windowsill. He got it at a Choctaw art fair out in Red Lick last May, just after he joined this jam band. Standard shakers are filled with sand, but this one's all mesquite seeds and screwbean pods. It sounds like wet nails, and he loves it. This song, "Orange Julius Caesar," requires him to play the same two-measure bassline seventy-eight times, so he steps on his sampler pedal, plucks the riff once, kicks the button, and the computer loops it for him. He needs his hands free to do other things, like shake the shaker, or drink bottles of Diet Mountain Dew, or put those bottles on his thumbs, but of course he doesn't do shit like that anymore.

"What's it mean," Cowboy Dan says, "if something is a meme?" He tells them about the library, and each member of Bitter Buffalo grabs an iPhone. Swipe. Click. They find it quickly.

"Well," Roberto says, giggling. "Aren't you?"

"Aren't I fucking what?"

"A player."

"A player?" Cowboy Dan says. "In the scene? I'd say so. I've been in—"

"I heard you were kicked out of this band," Gina says, pointing to her phone.

"I mean like a *player*-player," Roberto says, and Garrett adds: "And a brawler."

"Not anymore, man, you know me, the me *now*. And Gina—it fucking was amicable."

"I get it, we were born in different eras," Garrett says. "But I've heard some stories."

The room is quiet save for someone's amp sliding into feedback. Cowboy Dan grabs his bass. "You win, man. I'll go fucking easy on the shaker."

Cowboy Dan's done surf rock, garage, folk punk, blues, grindcore, and even, in a pinch, polka. Same digs. Same clubs. Same results. As long as everyone in the band is playing an *actual* instrument, he can get along. Cowboy Dan's analog. It took almost a decade for him to finally use the sampler pedal his pal Priscilla bought him for his fortieth. He used to get so bored playing the same surf rock riff over and over—one time he fell asleep on stage. Plus, he's off alcohol. And two summers back he flushed the last of his uppers, so he needs something to keep him busy, like the shaker, or like his favorite pastime: scanning the sea of people for a fan. Tonight it's not so much a sea as a drizzle, a puddle, a dozen people on devices.

All Cowboy Dan thinks he wants is—just once—to turn from his amp, stroll to the front of the stage, peer out into the audience, and find some people singing back the lyrics. He loves that shit, to be in an audience, yelling along to a song, like he and the band and everyone around is infected with the same virus. Usually he'll sing even if he doesn't know the lyrics, just sing his own ("My heart is not a mime, my heart is not a mine, my heart is not mine") to show his solidarity with the artists on stage. When you're playing music to a crowd who isn't singing back, who isn't even there—it's like you're infected all alone. There's no weirder feeling. And Cowboy

Dan's wasted enough of life feeling weird. He would love to just feel a little bit good.

Late September, Cowboy Dan opens his flip phone and calls his landlord to try one last time to convince him not to sell the spite house. The home is thin, unsafe, faded violet, stubborn, and tucked between two office buildings downtown. For two decades he and his landlord have stood strong against the offers of developers. In that time, the whole downtown rebirthed itself, nearly every building save for this ugly house. But last month Gary gave in—insurance will pay for his wife's double mastectomy, but they won't pay for reconstruction. "I need to be cash un-poor," he'd told Cowboy Dan over beers on the back porch, both of them gabbing and pacing, avoiding all the loose boards. "Need you out by December," he said. Gary used to be a cable guy before they all started cutting the cord. He was big into stand-up and went by Gary the Cable Guy.

"Knock, knock," Cowboy Dan says.

"Who's there?"

"What's another fucking café going to do for this town?"

"Not certain they're demoing the place—but if they do, I hear it might be a poke shop."

"For the card game? I thought that died off."

"You're thinking Pokémon, which is back in a big way, actually. It's on the phones now. I had a kid in my driveway yesterday trying to catch something called a Gengar. Sounded like an STD to me. Kid didn't laugh. Didn't even look up. I swear that generation can't connect for a second," Gary says. "But no, Dan. This is food. Poke is some kind of raw fish."

Cowboy Dan wants to argue with Gary, feels the tingle in his knuckles, the old vestiges of pugilism—but he stops himself. He thinks of Dad, dying in that trailer park on the Texas side of town, how he always whined, *The fucking city came to me!* and wishes he could kiss the man.

"I saw you on the internet today," Gary says.

"That's not me."

"That's pretty funny," Gary says. "I don't care who you are."

This is hurtful, is what Cowboy Dan lands on. On each site he registers as a new fake name. *Take it down.* His avatars remain a gray shape, or an egg, or a desert landscape. *This man's dead, it's not right.* Soon other avatars respond. They find more photos. *I'll fucking kill you punks.*

"The computers are for research, sir," the librarian says, "not starting wars."

If you pay him eighty dollars, fifty on low days, Cowboy Dan will climb to your roof and remove your ugly, obsolete satellite dish. He'll rip it out, toss it down to the lawn, and haul it away to the scrapyard. No matter he doesn't like heights. He does it because it's a service people will actually pay him to perform (unlike music), so he suffers the dizziness.

Today, on the roof of a Tudor just over the state line, inside a development called Minnow Brook, beside a development called Shady Space, Cowboy Dan sweats all over the wrench in his hand while a cadre of teenage girls goofs around down by the pool. Every so often they sneak sips from beer bottles hidden in a gym bag. Their laughter should be affirming to him—some people out there still like other people, still communicate with their bodies. Humans can relate to one another yet. When he glances down, the three of them are perched along the diving board, feet submerged, their backs to him. The board bends low, almost touching the water. But they're on phones. How are they all holding on?

Cowboy Dan's wrench slips out of his hand, slides down the shingles and ramps off, flipping through the air and into the pool. Not one of the three girls turns toward the sound.

"Sorry!" Cowboy Dan says, standing, squinting down at them. He'll never forget the first job he did with his father, Cowboy Daniel, on a roof in the suburbs. The owner of the house had pointed up at them, saying to his wife, *Look, honey, they sold the ranch and bought a wrench.* Cowboy Daniel kept spitting down onto the hood of their Eldorado. Cowboy Dan spit too.

"What?" says the middle girl on the diving board, pivoting her head but not her shoulders, lending him just one ear.

"About the wrench."

All three girls turn around and give a thumbs-up, except their thumbs are huge, brown, shining in the sunlight—topped with Lone Star bottles. They burst into laughter, fall into the pool.

"You're all fakes!" he says.

"Fakes!" they parrot back.

Cowboy Dan finishes the job by kicking the dish, just keeps kicking until it snaps.

Cowboy Dan doesn't drink anymore. Doesn't fight, doesn't fuck, hasn't pointed his pistol at anyone in years. He rejects that Dan wholly. He does, however, still drive out into the desert and fire Dad's rifle into the sky. He likes to stand still, waiting to see, hear, or feel the bullet fall.

Cowgirl Man does a dance down on Robison, by the college. She stands in the median, denim riding high, flannel shirt tied at the waist, ten-gallon hat slipping down over her eyes. The bass she wears is not plugged in. She marches, flipping batons and brown bottles high in the air and catching them. Cars honk, passersby laugh. She makes enough in tips the first week to pay her internet bill. The schtick gets old by week two, and the police ask for a permit.

The YouTube video ("Cowgirl Man's a Majorette") still hasn't taken off, and it's hot tonight, so her thumb gets stuck in the bottle. Her friend, filming, takes a hammer to it softly, tapping. It breaks. They scream. So much blood in her thumb, more than she ever knew. This clip becomes a GIF that grips the internet's eyelids. A metal band called Crisco Disco takes a grainy still of it for an album cover. Cowgirl Man is not credited. The album is a hit, but only in Australia. She cold-emails reporters in Austin, NYC, Sydney, begging them to tell her story.

Cowboy Dan was off-grid for the longest time, hiding from not only creditors, but also men who would want to exact revenge—*You beat up my brother. You slept with my girlfriend.* Now, with his face all over cyberspace and spilling out into the real world, he fully expects to have his door knocked down. The truth is that he almost wants it. The tension is one thing, but the solitude is another, so go ahead. Knock it down. Rip him out like a nail. Bring a fucking hammer.

It's October and Cowboy Dan's still writing '15 instead of '16 on his checks, which all bounce anyway. He falls asleep each night to the sound of running water. Not a tchotchke fountain or the rain or an ambient album set to repeat, but his toilet tank. It is always running, trying to fill. He loves the sound, can't sleep without the thin trickle through the wall. Best song he knows. He turns forty-nine on Christmas Eve.

"Don't fix it," Cowboy Dan tells Gary.

"I have to. I want to get every dollar I can out of this sale."

"They're just gonna level it, man. And I still don't know where I'm fucking gonna go."

"I'm shocked to hear it." Gary affixes a fishing sinker to the float ball and the trickle stops. Cowboy Dan kicks his shaker around like a soccer ball, filling the silent house with rattle.

"Well, you're goddamn famous," Gary says, crossing his eyes and giving Cowboy Dan a thumbs-up. "Go make some money off that."

"Tell me, where does one fucking go to collect his internet cash?"

"You don't feel any different? Any change at all? Now that everyone knows your face?"

"I feel the same as I did when I was six years old," Cowboy Dan says, lying.

"Dan fancies himself somewhat like the dude from that bowling movie about the pissed-on rug, except he's not a slob—no, this guy dresses to the western nines," says Priscilla, who was Cowboy Dan's closest friend until the night she told him he should give not-drinking a try, and his response was to try and kiss her, twice, and she kicked him out, kicked with her legs, her boots, but she doesn't tell the reporter this. "The fucking *nines*," she says, directly into the mic.

"Do you know the photographer too?"

"That's no photographer. That's a pornographer. And I'd love to shake their hand."

Cowboy Dan leaves the Novocain Stain at nine p.m., his belly one big wave of Mountain Dew. The engine of his '92 Silverado won't turn over, so he heads home on foot, his shaker in hand. If he were the younger Dan, he would meander, swervingly, down the sidewalks until he caught the eye of some punk who could make him turn the shaker into a weapon. But he is not that Dan. He's been to therapy, though not AA. Cold turkey was hard, but it took—he knows he's lucky. He's cried a lot. He gets the mechanics of meditation. He's been reading the forewords to Buddhist books. He's given up the hand on the knee in the dark of the bar. He hopes the people he's hurt have given up remembering, but doubts it. Walking home to the soon-to-be-ghost house, his body feels grainy, pixelated, like he's falling away to something not-him. Not-Dan.

A passing couple stares him down. The woman is dressed like a cockroach and the dude is him, is a Cowboy Man, down to the garnet bolo tie and the six-pack of Lone Star.

It's like the whole world is out there singing along to this song, *his* song, except the words were written by a stranger. Or by God. Or maybe he did write them.

"Heyo!" the passing man says, laughing, waving, giddy. "We're Cowboy Men!"

It's Halloween, and across the city, twenty-nine people have dressed as Cowboy Dan. Plus a few dozen more are Cowgirl Man, batons in bloody hands. In NYC, there are hundreds. LA reaches a thousand. In the tiny town of Kanorado, squatting on the border of two western states, there is a trio of young boys all dressed like Cowboy Man, pulling beer bottles out of a recycling bin, placing one on each of their fingers (the way Cowboy Daniel, stoned, used to do with Bugles) and chasing each other around the yard. Cowboy Dan does not know this. Nor does he want to. He wants to know that the world still has room for beauty, not just the echo of it.

"What's that even mean?" he says to the streetlight that his forehead is pressed against, trying to convince his heart that he's not drunk, his brain that he's not spinning.

Beneath his head is a flyer reading: "Have you seen this meme? I made it. It's mine," and at the bottom: "Pay me and I'll make you famous too. Nadine North—Ironic Photography."

Cowboy Dan rips the flyer in half trying to pull it off the pole.

On *The Daily Show*, a correspondent of the "Contemporary West" is dressed like Cowboy Man. The host sets up questions for him like T-ball. The actor playing Cowboy Man bunts all the jokes to the mound, yet the audience roars. Cowboy Dan doesn't get cable anymore.

The toilet fix took, and Cowboy Dan can't sleep with the silence. He rolls over and feels the flyer crinkle in his breast pocket. He reaches for the cordless phone, but he forgot to hang it up, so it's dead. Soon he's driving to the desert to take shots at the loud stars. Click, click. Out of ammo.

Back in his silent house, Cowboy Dan finds a 35mm photo of himself looking soberish at a party in 1999, tapes it to a piece of copy paper and writes in Sharpie: "I saw it. It's me," and walks to the Kinko's. He pins one up beside every copy of the meme-maker's flyer.

Cowboy Dab. Cowboy Damn Daniel. I don't always play bass guitar, but when I do take a power stance. I can haz Lone Star? All your bass are belong to him. Is the dress blue, black, or . . . paisley?

"This will never end," Cowboy Dan says, scrolling on Roberto's phone.

"This will never end," Roberto says to the rest of the band. They've been waiting and waiting to begin practice. They have a big New Year's gig and very few basslines written.

"This will never stop."

That night, Cowgirl Man makes a similar flyer, a sepia-toned photo of herself in The Pose—"But have you seen me? I'm more." Now every light pole along Hickory Street is ringed with the three flyers. The edges of each one touches the other two, forming a circle. It's mine. It's me. I'm more. You're mine. He's more. I'm her. Cowboy Dan will find this tomorrow and admit to no one but himself that it is beautiful, the way each paper's edge meets the next one, flush.

It's December and Cowboy Dan fits everything he didn't pitch into his truck and drives to practice. Not one amp is on before he's asked to leave the band. It's a walk he's done before. It's how he learned the meaning of *amicable*. He shakes Garrett's hand, Gina's hand, hugs Roberto. He tips his hat. The plane is definitely not crashing. He slings the bass over his shoulder, grabs his shaker, cocks back, and whips it at the window. The glass holds. The shaker cracks. What's inside are not beans or seeds, but fluorescent plastic beads, like a child's art project.

At the Novocain he unfolds the flyer in his pocket, asks to use the phone, and dials the meme-maker's number.

"It's you," Cowboy Dan says. They sit at a table by the pool tables. She is half his age.

"It really is," she says, holding out her hand. "I'm Nadi."

He lets her hand hang there. "Make it stop."

"I don't have that power."

"Listen, I'm not trying to shake you down for money."

"Money?"

"Profiting off my likeness."

Nadi hits her head on the wood wall behind her—that's how hard she laughs.

"I posted that thing on my blog six years ago, back when memes were funny, and art. Some bot account reposted it last May. Off it went. Sucked up into the tubes of the internet."

"Tubes?"

"And then you go and feed the trolls with your little posts."

"Trolls?"

"I haven't made a red cent, is what I'm saying. You think there's gold in the Web? People don't pay for entertainment. Don't you know that, mister musician?"

They watch the television in silence. It's a commercial for a show about a community of people living in tiny houses, but it's a contest, and each week one family loses, and their house is burned in front of them, while they watch. Cowboy Dan swears that one of the contestants is dressed as him. But maybe he's just dressed *like* him. Fuck. He's the problem. Him. Dan. Ego. He now sees every Stetson, every bass guitar, every bolo tie, as a refraction of himself.

Nadi taps a breakbeat on the table with her thumbs.

"Do you play?"

"Yeah," she says. "Well, a drum machine."

"Oh . . ."

"Jesus, tell me this: Who's paying all the old men of the world to be Luddites?"

"I'm not old."

"Of a certain age."

"Of a certain age, yes."

"Listen," Nadi says. "I know who my dad was, so don't worry, but my mom swore she slept with you, back in like '97."

"I'm sorry to hear that."

Nadi laughs, motions at the contestant on the TV show.

"I guess everyone has a piece of you."

"Everyone but me," Cowboy Dan says, shuddering at the gross poetry. Nadi pulls out her phone, types this down, a lyric she might use someday.

"Are you twittering about me?"

"Do you want me to?"

They take a selfie.

The spiral continues. A story appears in BuzzFeed called "The Year in Internet Memes," and soon some Hollywood producers fly to Arkansas. Nadi shakes hands with the first person to approach her. They find Cowboy Dan sleeping in the bed of his truck. The idea is this: ninety minutes inside the life of a meme. Netflix documentary. They'll manufacture a band just for the film. Cowboy Dan decides not to care. He consents. His hand is so cold that when he signs whatever they put in front of him, the signature is not his name—it's just marks, echoes of letters, lines, and lines.

Cowboy Dan and Nadi's drum-and-bass act goes over like an engine in Austin. They dress to the western nines and play grooves that bring the neon out in everyone. Dan makes faces only the camera can see. Cowgirl Man dances centerstage, strutting, marching, tossing her baton far into the dark of the rafters. On the new song, "Come Down (Too Soon)," she strings together so many somersaults that when she lands back on her feet it's tomorrow, and she's a different person altogether. And then it's tomorrow again, tomorrow again, until it's that lossy kind of tomorrow where you can't make out the edges of anything—and all of this no longer matters to anyone.

III

OF A WHOLE BODY
(PASSING THROUGH)

"Inhale and root yourself through your feet," says the yoga instructor. "Reach." And each resident reaches, forgetting to breathe. "Now, release and yearn your sternum forward."

"Did she say turn? Or yearn?" Eve whispers to Virgil, who slouches deep into the seat of his wheelchair. The CD in the stereo skips. "I don't think I know how to yearn my anything."

"And now," says the yoga instructor, "we're exhaling."

✳

At seventy-seven, Allan is the youngest resident of Ecumenica Assisted Living. His lone window looks out at the service lot—five spaces and a fence white with bird shit—so he spends most mornings in Marcia's room. She never speaks, but has the building's best view. Out across the one-lane road, the park trees tower and moms jog behind strollers and, just above the petting zoo fence: the alert ears of a llama. Allan's nurse, obeying the diet, forbids him coffee, but Marcia offers cold sips of hers. Allan offers his hand, which she evades. Instead, she reaches for his lap.

✳

Norma rejects the word *nurse*. These kids who push the chair while her knee heals, they're not nurses. They haven't gone to nursing school. Nurses have sass, might, wit, and far less sleep. She knows this, after a year in the hospital with Bob—nurses are nails. These dopes in their yellow polos blanch at a drop of coughed-up blood. *Nurses?* No.

At Wordshop, after the college student says to "meditate on dark blue," Norma pens her first complaint, sends it to the program manager. *Helper* comes next. Residents and helpers. *Only helper I need is hamburger,* she says, though her diet bars all nonwhite meat. *All they help is themselves to paychecks and Wi-Fi.* Eve, at a nearby table, adds: *If they want to help so bad, then hold the exits open so we can leave!*

Then, it's *handler.* That's what pushing a wheelchair is, right? Handling. Still, Norma objects. *Handle who? Me? You can't handle me—I'm a lion,* she says at Music Therapeutics, and then roars, scaring her handler. Her whole clique laughs. Tiny as it is, this matters to her. At eighty-six, what matters is a slippery slope. Never will she sigh, *It is what it is,* and let death off without a fight. *But seriously,* she says, *handler? I don't bite. These teeth ain't even real,* and she pops her top row out for effect, but also, she loves that suctiony sound, like a fridge door snapping open.

✳

Eve escaped once. Of course, words cause debate. To her it was *escape.* To Virgil, it was *a suicide attempt.* Norma went with *protest.* Allan, *an errand.* The program manager said it was *nothing to worry about.* Marcia had no comment. Eve got all the way to Lacuna Road, to the farmhouse where she'd lived after retiring from the school district, where she'd spent the last free years of her life alone. That is, until the court guardian appeared at her door with an order, signed by Eve's doctor and some judge, to take her to Ecumenica. The guardian showed photos of a mangled stop sign at the doctor's office, asked: *What if it'd been a stroller?*

The day Eve escaped back to her house, a prairie wind had shaken down a farmer's fence, and a herd of gray sheep flooded into the intersection of Lacuna Road and Victory Avenue. She heard their hooves knocking the asphalt as she found her home: solid and locked, empty but unsold.

Virgil does not want them to pray for his health. He does not want help designing an invitation for his ninety-third birthday. He does not want dessert. In a Christian sense, he loves them all, how they deliver him to activities as opposed to leaving him in front of a TV, but he wishes they would look the other way while he spits out his pills. *Ecumenical* means *of a whole body.* The physical body being only a single, diminishing piece. He wants to be believed when he says, *I want to die.*

The program manager invites Marcia to her office for a *chat.* Marcia is informed that Allan's warning signs have progressed into symptoms. Has she noticed? On the yellow legal pad in front of her, Marcia writes: *Cushions.* The program manager nods. "Yes, and *how* do you know he takes all the cushions from the lounge furniture, piles them on his bed, and then sleeps in the tub?" Marcia writes: *Beau.* "Right, you two have become close, and listen, Marcia, we think that's fantastic. Purpose. Companionship. It's what we're about. But you should know that . . ." and Marcia is told that she and Allan are forbidden to have sex. Sex. Because of his condition. Condition. His dementia. Dementia. Makes the issue of consent. Consent. Legally . . . tricky.

Plus, you know, his heart. Heart. Marcia writes on the pad: *No.* The program manager squints at the word, then at Marcia, and decides they are on the same page.

✳

If there's one thing the fifty-six residents agree on, it's that Cadet serves a purpose. Yes, it's annoying when he trespasses through the automatic doors, steps onto a café chair, and proceeds to shout about a past life. Yes, it's strange, his braided beard. And it's startling if your window faces east, toward the park, and, occasionally, Cadet comes into view, knocking on your window with a small stone, waving at his reflection to let him in. The crank calls get old. The theories get silly—that he lived here in the fifties when the building was a boarding school for Native children, an assimilation site, a place where, according to Eve, your life was beaten out and fed back to you by book; that his granddaughter is the program manager; that he lives in a trailer by the park, and cannot, due to his arrests or lack of funds, even make Ecumenica's waiting list.

But everyone quietly agrees on his significance: *At least I'm not that crazy.* This is especially so for those whose minds have become, not strangers, but quiet neighbors. They can hold eye contact with themselves in a bathroom mirror, sigh relief. *Help me want to keep my pants on,* says Allan to his handler. *Keep me a step above the Space Cadet,* who was once found in the F wing, nude from the waist down, singing.

✳

For about a week, the word *minder* catches on. *Mind? Huh? You think I don't have one of those?* Norma says. *I can mind me just fine. You mind your phone,* she says to Kirsten, her least favorite minder. The girl doesn't even have her bachelor's and smells of the mall.

Bob would've told Norma just to *mind* her own damn business—zip it. They could've argued this one for days. Disagreement was their pastime. Politics, thread counts, the color of a peacock, anything could fuel debate. They'd call friends separately to poll the subject, collect data for rebuttals based on popular opinion. They were unscientific, incensed, but attentive. Not once was a single issue settled, and it was perfect, the love of all those unresolved questions.

Finally, Norma calls them what they are: *employees of Ecumenica Assisted Living,* and still nobody gives her the fight she wants, so she uses *Ecumen,* or -man, for singular, which catches on—*Has anybody seen my Ecuman? My tomatoes in the garden need water.* For Kirsten, Norma's tempted to use *Ecugirl,* but instead she just shouts *Kirsten* as the crowd files into the sanctuary. *If I get a bad seat at church,* she says, pushing herself just fine, *I won't hear a word.*

Regardless of the weekly prompt the student brings to Wordshop, Eve writes about the day the Germans crossed the line. The soldiers took their farmhouse as an outpost, spared her family but moved them into the big gray barn with the animals. The soldiers—mostly boys under twenty—put her family to work because they didn't know how to make sauerbraten that tasted like memory, or how to hold a needle to their tattered coats. Ewa, age eight, remembers this most, working so diligently in the barn's cold loft to sew buttons on a vest. She wanted her work to be perfect, hoping those boys might appreciate her craft, obedience, possibly even her grit, and eventually invite her back into the house to sleep in her room again.

She'd scrub the floors free of marks left by their boots, which they never removed—she could still hear them stomping. Never did she think about escape.

She swore to never make that mistake again.

✳

One day, by the Computer Café, a great glass enclosure appears. Dozens of birds, varying in size, color, and vocal register, hop from branch to plastic branch in a kind of constant frenzy. "Yellow birds, red birds, orange, gray. White ones with hairdos," Allan says, passing through.

"But why no blue ones?" he later thinks aloud, as the program manager, leading News on This Day, asks if they want to discuss: Teddy Roosevelt's trip to Panama (1906), Kristallnacht (1938), Opening the Berlin Wall (1989), or the IRS's seizure of Willie Nelson's assets (1990).

"It's all warm colors, but nothing cool," Allan says to Marcia, beside him. She puts a finger to her lips. "You can break a sweat just looking at the cage. Can we get some blue?"

"You know what?" says the program manager, looking up from the article. "There just aren't a lot of natural things that are blue. Meaning, like, in nature, blue is very rare."

"Whoever told you that never looked up," Norma says. "Hello—sky?"

"There's nothing actually blue about the sky," says the manager. "It's more a reflection."

"Right," Eve says. "Because water is blue."

"Water is not blue," Virgil says, holding up his glass, which is still full, because he did not need it to wash down his pills after he successfully spit them out behind the couch.

"Water is *so* blue!" Eve says, prepared to prove it.

"Have you seen the Minnesota River?" Norma says, switching sides. "Its color is *mud*."

"What I'm saying is that blue almost never appears on animals, plants, land."

"Blue jays, bluebells, Blue Earth County," Norma says.

"Enough," the program manager says. "We'll look into getting a blue bird for the aviary."

Allan raises a hand. Though no one calls on him, he says, "You ever seen a purple one?"

No, Marcia writes. Shaking her head will no longer suffice. She must write it down, underline it. Because this is not his first proposal, nor will it be the last. The thing is: marriage means a wedding, government, money, another military funeral. And why spend any more of what's left of her life disappointing someone and then watching him die? She just wants to spend her mornings looking out the window beside this handsome man, this man who makes her feel new every time he gathers her breasts into his hands. She underlines *No* a second time.

Allan closes the invisible box on the invisible ring, and staggers back to his feet.

Touch me, Marcia writes. And outside, pulling bags of birdseed from her trunk, the program manager notices Allan obeying.

No one agrees on the birds. Or the cage. The pro-bird residents argue it isn't even a cage. Some love the sight of it. Some, the sound. Some, familiar with the article taped to the library door, accept the birds for purely practical reasons—life extends life, and a few ferns do not suffice. Others see cruelty, want the birds freed, prefer to find them brown and unimpressive, right outside their windows, crowding a feeder but welcome to leave. Some say these exotic birds wouldn't make it on their own, out there in December, in Minnesota. What about winter? The cold? Surely an orange chick smaller than a scone could not make it all the way south. Some would like to see the creatures spill out into hallways and find their way home, but no one would ever take action the way Cadet will, one cold November morning, charging into the building past the distracted Ecupeople to smash the glass with a rock. Everyone will agree it was quite a sight, all those creatures careening for the door. Everyone, that is, but Allan, who will be nearest to the glass, admiring the new blue thrush when it happens, and who will watch that bird writhing on the carpeted floor, a shard stuck far into its feathers.

✳

When the students realize that volunteering to lead Wordshop does not count toward school credit, they stop showing up. "I'm sorry to say," the program manager tells the five still-dedicated writers gathered in the library, "but this activity is on hiatus for now."

"What?" Norma says. "You can't give us something to write about?"

"I'm not exactly a writer."

"What about the internet? Look one up? Ask Kirsten here, she's online as we speak."

The program manager turns to Kirsten, who stumbles, but only for a moment. "Um, okay," she says, reading. "Write about your life, as a movie? I mean, like, who would play you?"

✳

In B wing, a dull blue sign reads DAYS SINCE LAST ACCIDENT: 0. Eve is convinced that there is blue outside, too. If she could take one of her old walks, she'd find the blue. There was blue, blue *something*, growing in the brush behind the house on Lacuna. Maybe she'd bring some back to end that argument still happening in her head. Or maybe she wouldn't. Maybe she'd keep on walking, right past the house, toward something else entirely.

She makes a course down the hall with her walker, all the way to the unmanned security desk. She peeks over, looking for keys, but sees a news clipping with a sticky note that says WHY WE MUST DO BETTER. It's a back-page story from the local paper, dated months ago, telling of an elderly woman who fled Ecumenica and made it all the way out to the prairie. At first Eve is grateful that the writer didn't name her, but then again, maybe she'd like some credit.

In Marcia's room there's a small photo of a man petting a horse. He looks like a hippie. So, after a month of wondering why she won't marry him, Allan decides he'll start wearing his hair long. Being career Army, he's never in his life felt his hair touch his ears. At his appointment, he tells the traveling barber: "You know what, Helen? Just wash it. No trim for me. Can we just wash it and say you cut it? Can you do that for me, Helen?"

"Yes sir, Mr. Allan, but my name is Cathy."

Each month he savors the way her fingers probe his skull, the spruce and cucumber shampoo, the small talk. The wash and dry takes five minutes, tops. With all the time left over, Allan and the barber chat about Marcia, or sometimes his ex-wife, Helen, and he can feel it, his hair growing.

*

At Lifelong Learners, the middle-aged man controlling the slideshow praises the amazing advances of 3-D printing. "This is a 3-D printed carpal trapezium," he says, pointing to his palm.

"Oh, perfect," says Norma. "Can you print me a new Ecugirl?"

Her audience laughs. The man does not. "I'm sorry?" he says.

"Me too," Norma says, turning toward the corner where Kirsten sits.

"When the hell are you going to leave me alone?" Kirsten says, silencing the room.

Norma thinks she sees tears in Kirsten's eyes, but maybe it's glitter from her eyeshadow.

"What'd I ever do to you?"

"Finally," Norma says. "I get a little rise out of you."

✳

On the coldest morning of the year, there appear in the sky three separate hazy suns. One bright and round like a flashlight through a bedsheet; two dimmer slivers on either side. It's as if a giant eye has opened up. "My barber says it's called a sundog," Allan tells Marcia, as she runs her fingers through his hair. Over by the park, they see Cadet in gym shorts, shoveling snow.

Tomorrow they'll move Allan up to the Memory Wing, where the nurses are actual nurses, where there's no dining hall because all the food's delivered, where a single cold symptom turns the whole hall into a quarantine, and Marcia will map a path there. She'll wake early, pack a thermos, and try and fail and try again to make the elevator move without a key.

✳

The program manager asks them to write about what they want from the New Year. Resolutions, goals, keep it positive. Only Virgil writes of hope for death. "It's the same resolution every January, and I never get it crossed off the list, but finally, I want to die," he says—and he will, in February, with pneumonia, after leaving his bedroom window open night after night after night.

"Thank you all for sharing," the program manager says. "Now let's prepare to transition."

"What do we do now?" says Eve.

"Next, I believe, is Wii bowling."

"No, I mean, now," she says, holding her paper up in the air like a flag. "With this story."

"I'll type it. Then we'll put it in your binder so you have all your writings in one place."

"What do *I* do with it," Eve says. "What do I do to get it in the paper?"

"The actual newspaper? The *Mankato Free Press*?" Norma asks and begins to laugh.

"Well," the program manager says. "I don't know if this is something the paper—"

Eve tears the paper from her notebook, folds it in half, and rises to her feet.

"I know an easier way to get your name in the paper," Norma says, tilting her head to the right, rolling back her eyes, sticking out her tongue. "They call it the obit—"

"—Shut up, Norma," Kirsten says. The room is silent until Norma smiles warmly, then everyone starts talking at once, each with their own opinion.

Eve hears none of them as she inches her way toward the place where she will go at the close of every Wordshop from now until her death—the mailroom. Every story she sends to the paper is a part of her escaping. A small part, but enough.

✳

"My movie was straight to TV, late to the producers, and somehow still way over budget. No one saw it. A knockoff Mary Pickford, that's who plays me. My movie airs on Channel 11, late, Tuesday nights, and it's that thing from the seventies how at midnight the national programming stops, just the American flag waving over the anthem," says the program manager, sharing Marcia's page aloud above the sound of the crowd's laughter at a community reading held in the sanctuary. *"My life, now just those colorful bars and that noise."*

And everyone present makes the noise, each note uniquely flat and belonging to no scale.

MIDTOWN

The poet mopped the floor with us. The poet opened up like a cornered sky and fell on us. The poet felled us. The lights flickered. No drinks were ordered. Nobody rose for the pisser. The poet, a warned-about force, put everything internal up for sale—for free, on the front porch of their voice—and we carried all we could handle home. For days we walked slower for how the poet made us feel about trees. We just needed to touch every trunk, rub the leaves, smell our hands, compose dark, sloppy emails about how it all felt—emails we then sent to the poet, who never responded, but did post online that they were not in a good place, mentally, and then apologized for transgressions no one in the poet's life remembered.

A picture of our sorry faces was taken for the paper, and the headline said: THE TOPS OF THESE PEOPLE'S HEADS HAVE BEEN TAKEN OFF BY A POET, and of course we read the article, shared it, clipped it out, pinned it up at work, and watched it watch us wither, all the while turning over the article's pull-quote: "I think a poem is a dig site. I'm talking archaeological. There's some shit down there," the poet said, "and I just want one other thing on the record. I'm sorry I couldn't get through the book signing without crying. I don't know what's wrong with me."

We promised our loved ones—though later, of course, we failed—that we would never forget how the poet had trounced us. The night of the reading we'd eaten dinner early, or out, or alone as usual, just to be on time for our trouncing. After all, we had come to be trounced, and we had been, had been hurt well and good, had been dunked on. We had, by the poet, been altered.

Our hands still sting from the applause.

We didn't know when to clap, and then—we didn't know when to stop.

WHERE THE RUBIES LIVE

The night before I became a failed salesman, I was wired and awake in Derek's room, gazing out his window, reading his anatomy textbook, and eating peanut butter with a knife. I had questions—big questions—but it was two a.m., and all my older brother cared about was getting sleep. If every hour we lose hair and grow cells and our bones thicken overnight, are we different people the next morning? Derek grunted in the negative. Never had he felt his arms grow longer, no matter how new he looked to me every time he emerged from the pool, fists up in victory.

What I loved most about going to meets was his starting-block routine, a series of stretches I knew by heart. I'd repeat after Derek as he moved pieces of himself—slow head roll, delt shrug, arms to heaven, finger wiggles, bow at the waist, hammy stretch, ankle arch, toe curl, ending with a ten-step run-in-place. Up on those metal bleachers at ten years old, it wasn't swimming I cared about. It was the idea that my arms might grow long enough to reach all the way down there and tap him, just before the whistle blew, on the shoulder.

That night I stood at his window, stretching. "Want some Jif?" I said, offering the knife.

"Jesus, Bret," he said. "Go to bed." This was when Jesus was no longer a swear, after Dad joined TEAM and traded Sunday service for sales trips. It was after we'd moved uphill.

"Relax," I whispered. "We don't have anywhere to be tomorrow, right?"

As Saturday night wobbled into morning, I stared down the hill at the lights along the dog-food factory—gold, red, some even emerald, like the jewels I somehow believed my dad sold door to door. I tried to remember what life was like when we lived down there but my brain dug up so little. Besides, it made much more sense to focus on the future, who I was becoming.

Of course, now that I'm grown, all I ever think about is the past.

On the floor of Derek's room, I awoke in a diamond of sunlight. He stood at the long mirror, yanking at the cuffs of his suit jacket, trying to make them reach his wrists.

"Why are we dressing up?" I asked, hoping for church. I knew it was a thing of the past, but I missed the little cups of grape juice, the colorful windows, the way time stood still.

"Your brother's showing his first plan today," Dad said, coming in to organize Derek's hair with the harsh black comb. "He's joining TEAM." My brother's face said pain, each stroke ripping out something little but essential.

"His suit's too small," I said. No one listened to me. With his wingspan wide, Derek's arms rolled in tiny circles. My brother was a swimmer, not a salesman. I, however, felt I knew exactly how to woo. My school counselor wrote that I was "quite charming one-on-one."

I showered quick so that Dad wouldn't yell about wasted water, pulled on my polo, and even brought him the little evil comb to make my hair successful. I stood in the kitchen, waiting to be preened. Dad swallowed coffee and said, "You'll show the plan once you're older."

"That's what you said about playing drums in praise and worship band," I said. "And now we don't even go! Who knows what this family will be doing when I'm old enough?"

"Okay, Bret," Dad said, his eyes shut tight like my voice hurt. "There's no room—"

"—in this house for gloom," I said. "I know. But this isn't gloom. This is the truth. Promises suck, because no one knows if the future me will want the things the me today wants."

"See what I mean?" Derek said to Dad. "He's nine going on Nietzsche."

"I'm ten!" I said, as Dad shrugged and flipped open his cell phone to make a call.

"Dude, go make some friends today," Derek said. "Have fun while you still can." He was talking to me, but looking somewhere else, somewhere inside the folds of his growing brain.

"Or go get some exercise," Dad added, closing the phone.

My family thought I was the only one who didn't notice my own fat. They'd accuse me of eating saltine sleeves, spaghetti leftovers— but that was Derek, bulking up for meets. I watched him trying to drink coffee, how he just held it in his mouth. And here I could drink coffee fine. Actually, I loved coffee and could even tell you what the chemical caffeine does to our bodies—the molecule looks like a dead frog. It's pictured in Derek's Bio book. Dad ran his pinky along the inner lip of a Jif jar, a habit Mom hated. He leaned toward me—*Shhhh*—and popped the finger into his mouth.

"Okay, but who could turn down a cute kid?" I said. "You'll sell like a hundred rubies with me there, smiling and making jokes." The men of my family laughed at me.

"You have no idea what you're talking about," Dad said. "Besides, I've got the cute kid strategy already working." He clapped my brother's back, and Derek spit coffee onto the floor.

"Jesus," Dad said, inspecting his shirt for stains. We stood still in the kitchen, all of us hungry, listening to the faint sound of Mom in the side yard, singing to her vegetables.

Across the garden, Mom knelt by her pepper plant, gloveless and already sweaty. I wanted to know why I couldn't go. She looked into the sky as if Dad was a planet you could sometimes spot in daylight. The station wagon left the driveway without even a honk goodbye.

"It's too early to get worked up," she said. The strip of yard between our house and the neighbor's fence was a tunnel of flora. Snap peas sprouted along the fence, baskets of herbs hung from the gutters. Every part of a salad grew in disorderly islands, a logic only Mom knew. I picked my way through the plants, moving toward her voice. She was out here for hours every morning. The grocery store she'd managed had been bought out back in June. I didn't understand how that had affected our family budget, had no concept of debt. Waiting for the bus each morning, I'd see Mom sitting beside the tomato wire, eyes squinted, watching for growth.

"Seriously," I said to her. "I can sell as much jewels as them."

"*Many*," she said. "And what do you mean, jewels? You don't even know the plan, Bret."

"I can learn. I learned about cells just last week. They're all over us, always multiplying and dying and coming off on our bedsheets. And remember, you taught me a cucumber was a pickle. All I need is someone to tell me. Give me a date then. When can I be on TEAM?"

"A cucumber isn't exactly a pickle. And it's not my job to tell you everything. Some stuff you have to figure out for yourself." She tried to hand me a trowel. "Listen," she said, whispering like she was telling a secret. "You won't like the TEAM. I mean, I can hardly stand them myself. The product they sell is always changing, and the people are so . . . flimsy."

Once a week she played N64 with me upstairs while the local TEAM members gathered in our living room to read aloud from a glossy book called *SELLEBRATE*. The cover showed a has-been pro wrestler leaning on the hood of a Lamborghini while a briefcase by his feet spewed golden light. I could never hear exactly what they were saying down there during the meetings, but talk always circled back to who's got silver, who's gone gold, where the rubies live, how hard a diamond is. "I bet you I'd love it," I said to Mom.

"Bret, honey," she said, sounding tired. "I'm sorry, but I have work to do here."

"Me too," I said, charging back across her garden, stomping through our family's food.

I searched the house for my mother's TEAMate, the requisite gray briefcase. She'd never even gone on a sale, so it would still be full of the product and the plan. After ten minutes of rummaging, I found it below the sink, a silver case branded with the gold TEAM logo. I imagined the shining things inside but, to my mind, had no time to look. I had to out-earn my father, sell better than my brother, and I had to start now. I threw open the front door and ran, my toes pressing up against the tips of my shoes.

I marched through our uncut, buggy grass, and into the street where I was nearly hit by a minivan. They laid on the horn, but I kept my head down, sun all over the back of my neck.

I rehearsed lines I'd overheard Dad and his TEAM repeat as I approached the stoop of the Clays' house, catching myself in the reflection of the glass door. My hair, a black sea in a storm. Lips chapped. Eyes bloodshot and wide open. Would I frighten my customers?

Then, a voice above my head that was not God's said, "Is that Bret frickin' Giatrini?"

Josh Clay's head jutted from the window, hovering above me, his acne sloppy as bridge graffiti. I coughed. "Hello, sir. May I have a minute with your family?"

"This shit again?" he said. "We already told your brother Derelict—we're not buying."

"Well, tell me this," I yelled up. "Do you ever dream of being your own boss?"

He hocked a loogie, and I was off, briefcase over my head like a shield.

As Josh's laugh died behind me, I chose a random house with a wraparound porch. The heavy knocker hung just in reach, made a solid rap. I cleared my throat and hummed a song Dad often belted in the shower while I failed to sleep—*Eye of the tiger, it's the thrill of the fight*. No one came to the door, so I pressed the bell. Its bright ring echoed through the house forever.

I wondered if each echo of the doorbell was the same or a different sound. How changed were they from the original ring? I thought of the Bret I'd been last night, then the Bret I was in the shower, the Bret falling through Mom's garden. Was I becoming Bret faster or slower than Derek had become Derek? I wiped the sweat growing inside my elbow-pits and imagined whole teams of cells flooding away. Is this porch the same now that I'm all over it? I stepped to the left, then to the right, trying to see if each move was the birth of a new Bret. Who was the true Bret?

"That's a neat little dance," said an old lady at the end of the porch, and I froze. She smiled wide—her teeth didn't quite fit her mouth—and pulled open the door.

Inside, she sat on a chair, but I stood. My voice, my pitch, the plan—
it echoed through her quiet house. I made everything up. Something
about jewelry, how you can buy silver and with enough work, you can
grow it into gold. Rubies and emeralds were next, I was pretty sure, and
the ingredients to grow these were Time and Faith. Love. Patience. Grit.
I mixed what I'd heard from our living-room TEAM meetings with
what I recalled from church, sprinkling in lines from my counselor's
cat posters—*Yesterday you said tomorrow, today just say MEOW!*

"Then, the creator comes down, wearing a crown of diamonds,"
I said, ready to open the briefcase. She smiled, staring past me with
shaky eyes.

"Bret-hunny," she said. "I get it."

"And that's when, I'm pretty sure . . ." I was trying hard to close,
hungry for the time to come when she handed me money, when I
slammed the dollars down on our dinner table, when Salesman-Bret
got all the praise he deserved. "—we're allowed into heaven."

"Turn around," she said, her voice now cutting like a thorn.
"Look at my bookshelf." Behind her were twelve identical spines—
SELLEBRATE—all in a row. "I'm already in your father's downline,"
she said. "He and that Derek are such nice young men. But, shhh,
I'm in a lot of folks' downlines," she said. I'd heard the word *downline*
before but never understood it. None of this made any sense. I sat
down. My hands shook, the briefcase rattling. She knew who I was?
Dad and Derek had been here? And how many times? "I heard the
Johnsons are going sapphire," she hissed.

When she asked if my dad knew I was here, I stood up to go.
She moved toward the phone, blocking my way to the front door.
"Shouldn't we call him?" she said, and her top row of false teeth
slipped out of her mouth. They smacked the floor, sounding like
knuckles cracking.

I screamed and bolted—briefcase held tight to my chest—down the hall, through a kitchen, out a door, and into the backyard. And beyond that, the woods.

I cut through the trees, my briefcase heavier with every step. These woods should've been the same that ran behind our house, but everything looked weird—the trees were shorter, more packed together, and the leaves seemed greasy, sticky. It was all downhill. I didn't know my way. I used rocks to cross a stream but landed in some black muck that sucked the shoe from my foot. My hair caught burrs and bugs as I waded through bushes. A branch tore a hole in my polo, right above my nipple. My eyelid bled from a briar scratch. I walked so long the shadows shrunk.

I must've looked deranged, because screams rang out the second my feet touched cut grass. Three young girls sat inside the empty body of a hot tub, pointing at me, shaking their heads *no*. I wanted to turn back but how would I find home through those trees?

"My daddy will kill you!" yelled the girl with beaded braids. She was the smallest, brown-skinned and squinting. Her left front tooth was gone, the new growth just a crooked stub.

"You're bloody," said the second, her freckles alive with sunburn. "Where's your shoe?"

"Is the road up that way?" I asked, licking my lips. At the top of the embankment, dumpsters overflowed with furniture, garbage. The sluggish Conewago Creek trickled behind us.

"We'll tell you if you help us," said the third, oldest girl. Her dark skin seemed to glow in the sun, and her blue bikini top made me queasy. "What do you know about hot tubs?"

I wiped my briefcase in the grass and said, "What I know about is jewel—"

But the middle one cut me off: "We need a plan for getting this thing into the creek." She jumped out and stood in front of me, squaring her shoulders. The other two followed suit.

"Why would you want to do that?" I said.

"So we can all float around in a freaking hot tub," said the oldest. "Duh."

"It's called living your best life," said the middle girl.

"What's in your case?" said the youngest, her braid-beads clicking together in the wind.

I decided to skip the speech and go right to the product. The bikini girl looked old enough for a weekly allowance. Maybe the youngest still got tooth fairy money. "Okay," I said, laying the briefcase flat in the grass. The girls came close. We formed a circle around the case, looking down as if into a hole that reached the other side of earth. I could not wait to finally show someone what I had inside. "Now, what I'm about to present to you," I said, unlatching the case. "You should picture it around your neck. In your ears. On your wrists."

The girls touched each other's arms. I held my breath and lifted the lid like a veil.

Inside, eight silver knives gleamed in the sunlight. The glare shot into our eyes, and my heart became a garden on fire, beds burning, tomatoes melting. The older girls cursed, sprinted up the hill—but the littlest smiled, looked right at me, and asked, "Can I do the next part?"

She chose the biggest blade and held it between us like night had fallen, the knife a torch. I thought about how I'd learned in Derek's textbook that two touching objects never actually made contact, how a tiny space always hovered between the electrons of each item. I couldn't say where we were, but inside I knew—this was the edge of our old neighborhood.

"Give me your shoe," she said, and I kicked it off. With that knife in her hand, I would've done anything she said. I had no confidence. I was a failure. I didn't even know the product.

She knelt down and commenced sawing my shoe clean in half. In a deep voice, she said: "As you see, it moves clean through the toughest stuff: meat, leather, even bone. This blade is reinforced steel, with a full tang, and three brass rivets that store-bought knives lack. This handle will *never* separate from its blade. It simply does *not* wear out! And it comes with our Forever Guarantee, which means regardless of time, use, and your ever-changing life, you'll never be without."

"You're good at this," I said, suddenly wanting a knife of my own. Or maybe I just wanted her to put that one down.

She continued in her husky, affected voice: "Now if you have a penny, I'd like to show you what the scissors can accomplish."

I picked up a knife and started into the inch-thick plastic hot tub liner. The blade cut with ease. The girl's name was Kiana. Her dad sold these too.

With knives long as our forearms, we sliced into the hot tub. "This is how you get the hot tub into the creek," she said. "One tiny piece at a time." Her laugh was catching, hoarse like Derek's, but not mocking.

"At that point, will it even be a hot tub anymore?" I asked, looking up the hill. The sun hung high in the sky. There was plenty of time left in the day, enough time for Kiana and I to make ourselves rich.

Forget the plan, whatever it'd been. These knives were divine, and the new plan was to sell them. I examined one as we walked, how it glinted, glowed, the handle so sturdy. I wondered if this was where the jewels were—melted down, remade into this. If so, were they still jewels? Was this a diamond or a knife? Was I still working for TEAM, or had I quit altogether?

At the corner of two streets I'd never seen, the stop sign was missing. The pole just stood there, crooked in the dirt, with nothing to show. Maybe it was because Kiana chose to hold my briefcase, but I suddenly felt nervous, like I was being tricked. I remembered the old woman with all her book copies, how she smiled after the teeth fell, the black hole of her mouth. I thought of Dad and Derek's mocking laughter. Everyone took me for an idiot.

Was I being robbed here? "Excuse me." I said. "Can I carry my briefcase?"

"Chill, I told you my dad used to sell Cutlass," she said. "What? You don't trust me?"

She sighed and sat in the dirt beside the curb. When she opened the briefcase and took out the hefty kitchen shears, I could feel my heart thumping through my stomach. "Blood brothers or soul sisters?" she said. I stared at her until she decided on soul sisters. She handed me the scissors, and demanded that I snip off a piece of hair. "Wake up!" she yelled, clapping her hands at my face. The shears, heavy in my hand, shook like a light about to go out. I imagined standing here with Kiana, taking turns poking at my severed ear on the curb. But when the blades touched a tuft of my bangs, the hair came off without a sound.

I cupped the black shreds in my hands.

"Give me," Kiana said, so I dumped the thin pile into her hand, and she pushed my hairs into her shorts pocket. She took the scissors, and in a blink she lopped off a whole braid, complete with the little green heart bead. She put it in my hand. "Okay, now we're bonded."

"Forever?" I said.

*

Passing stoops, birds, barbeques, and men gazing into the open hoods of bright cars, we sold to no one. Kiana led us in her big, silver flip-flops. The thong kept popping out of the left one, and we'd pause while she fixed it. I carried the suitcase, chin up, no smile, just like she instructed. A scent I knew blew through the air, a smell like Cheerios left too long in the bowl. We passed the smokestacks of the dog-food factory, but still I didn't recall this place as home.

At the park, teenagers sat on bleachers. Teenagers smoked by bathrooms. Teenagers did wheelies. Teenagers with shoulder muscles and mustaches ran across two netless basketball courts. Kiana navigated the landscape, confident and quick, graceful even with her flip-flops slapping. I jogged to keep up, looking around for seven-year-old me, as if past selves just stayed where you left them. The first group we met—four boys leaning on BMX bikes—glared at us.

I was silent. Kiana tried. "You guys need any—"

"Fuck outta here with that shit," the tallest one said.

The second group kept turning Kiana's questions back on us.

"Why you hanging with tubby here? Where the fuck his shoes at?"

"I'm trying to talk business," she said. I held tight to her braid in my pocket.

"I'm trying to talk about why you're out here with Ralph Lauren." He leaned close and flipped my collar up. His crew roared. We left, and Kiana welcomed me to Logan Park.

At the drink fountain, I let the water fill my mouth and spill over. I wet my whole face while Kiana shared with me her father's mantra which was: *Selling is cellular. It's in our blood.* She said her dad was so dedicated to his business that he left to live with other sellers in a neighborhood up the hill. He'd been a delivery driver, but was fired for selling the plan while making deliveries. Her dad had worked nights, a rotation between second and third shift, just like my dad used to do. She and I bonded over being woken up by our fathers leaving late at night, the car engine firing, the front door falling closed. Dinners were lonelier too. Now, even with my dad working first shift, he still missed dinner often. He always left to sell the plan. Because of this, Mom had a rule that everyone had to be home for Sunday dinner. I looked up at the sun, wondering if I'd be back up the hill and seated at our table in time.

Kiana stood up and started walking in circles, waving her hands as she lectured. "Dad says there's two kinds of people: ones who think the world is all buyers or sellers, and ones who know that if you're selling the right product, the buyers can become sellers too." I laughed, and she clapped her hands three times. "Listen, first we sell the knife—easy. But *then* we sell them tools for how to sell their own knives. And *then*, every time they sell a knife, we get cash, 'cus we brought them in." She took a deep breath and grabbed the suitcase. "*That's* the plan."

"So what you're saying is we make fishers of men," I said, but she was already walking.

Our first sale came near the bike racks, when a kid ran past us, nearly in tears, asking if we'd seen a guy with a beard riding a blue Huffy. Out of breath, he sat on the bench. Kiana skipped the pitch and struck. She popped the briefcase, and placed it on his lap.

"First-time customer," she said. "Special deal. Any of these for ten dollars."

As the kid slowly reached for one, I wondered: What if he turns it on us? But Kiana had it covered. She picked one up under the guise of showing him the rivets.

"Who are you?" he asked, running a finger along the handle. "Why do you have these?"

"We're your *team*," I said, grinning. Kiana's moxie had restored my will to sell. "We'll teach you to sell these, put you in our downline. You'll make back all your money."

"A hundred times," Kiana added. The kid pulled a Velcro wallet out of his pocket and handed me a ten-dollar bill. He took the smallest knife—the parer, Kiana called it—and slipped it into his pocket. Kiana put her hand out to shake, but the kid just walked away. She quickly sold another in the girl's bathroom while I struck up a too-slow conversation at the vending machines. The group there squinted at me, and when I mumbled something about knives, they smacked the briefcase out of my hands and demanded I go home.

"People want to feel big," Kiana said. "Safe and strong. Simple as that."

The shears went to a pair smoking behind the tennis court. The steak knife brought in five, plus half a PB&J sandwich, but the buyer—he wore a big black raincoat and kept arguing with himself—was like everyone else we'd sold to: He wouldn't sign up, didn't want in on our team. But he did shake my hand, and for a second we traded cells.

All day long I had been saying goodbye to tiny parts of me. I thought I was shedding an old Bret to make way for the new one— the salesman, the charmer, the pride of my clan.

Kiana tore the sandwich in half and we ate in the shade of a boarded-up concession stand.

After finishing the sandwich, my stomach hurt with hunger. And when a group of kids in green bandanas arrived, I wished I was at the house, bugging Mom while she prepped dinner. These kids had hard arms and wide shoulders like Derek. I elected not to offer a handshake.

"Heard you got blades," the biggest one said. What we had left were the two largest ones—serrated, silver, the length of a thigh, the kind of knives you might use to strip the skin from a fish, or saw through bone. I tried to smile, but the group gave back only hard stares.

"Well?" said one, his bandana like a scarf. I prayed silently and clutched Kiana's braid.

"Well?" Kiana said. Her tough tone slipped, her voice retreating to a younger version.

"Show us the goods."

"You got no money and you know it," she said. And with that, someone shoved me to the ground. In a blink they had the briefcase. *Peace!* they yelled, marching away. Kiana ran after them, and suddenly I was alone. I found a place beneath the bleachers and sat down in the dirt. I thought of Derek, always sure of his body and where it was headed. To the end of the lane, back. Repeat until varsity. Same person in a different place. I wanted to be home. But hadn't I lived here, once, in this neighborhood? I looked around again for our old house. I'd swung from those monkey bars, I swear, but Derek was always with me. I was never allowed at the park alone. Or was it a different park? What good was memory if it was always coming off in chunks?

"It's okay," I said when Kiana returned, red-faced and cursing. "We still got the money."

"But what about the plan? What about tomorrow?"

Kiana believed we'd be the same people tomorrow. But I thought I'd change when I showed the cash to my family. *Look at what I did for you, without you.* I couldn't wait.

"I'll get more," I told her. "We'll go out again next weekend. Try a new neighborhood?" She wouldn't look away from where the thieves had disappeared into the park's long shadows. "Where do you live?" I asked. "So I can come find you next time."

"Listen," she said, finally facing me again. "You can't tell my mama we done this. She hates this stuff. She kicked Dad out the house. She says the TEAM is a cult."

"What's a cult?"

"It's when you get so excited about something that someone ends up *killed*." The word hovered between us, and I think we understood something about what we'd just done. In fact, a boy Derek's age would soon be stabbed right here in this park. Not to death, but enough to stain the asphalt on the ball court so dark that a nearby church would pay to paint the whole court blue. Enough to warrant an investigation, a lawsuit, a settlement, an unalterable change in me I still can't name.

Kiana looked up, sucked in her tears, and straightened her spine. "Matter of fact," she said, shoving my arm. "You can't tell *anyone* about this."

I nodded, despite the fact that I was going to have to lie to someone—either to Kiana by breaking her promise, or to my parents by not telling the truth about the work I'd done, the money I'd made, the success I'd gained. It was not triumph I felt when Kiana handed me my half of the cash, but betrayal. Maybe this was my first inkling of the truth about adulthood: it's not an act of physical change, but a process of learning how to hide who you are, who you've been.

As we walked the streets in silence, I tried to memorize every sign and corner. I thought I'd be making my way back there soon. When she veered toward the stoop of a row house without a goodbye, I wanted to cut all the rest of my hair off and give it to her. I grabbed at the bounty in my pocket—twenty bucks and a girl's braid. The sun set fast, the sky a smoky pink. In the threshold, she turned to back to me, waved her arm through the twilight and yelled, "Go!"

*

At the foot of the hill, the hot tub sat there, unmoved. I closed my eyes and began to climb. Through the dim forest I soon saw my shoe stuck in the mud, but I left it. My feet had hardened. Alone now, I could think only of my family. What would they say when I got home? As I walked, my imagination built a table piled with the bounty of my mother's garden, me opening the door, my back straight, no blood on my face, the hole in my shirt stitched, my shoes clean and gleaming, my hands not trembling, and I drop it all into the center of the table, the money and the braid, right there on the Mount Rushmore placemat. I say, *We're getting ice cream tonight.* They gasp. *I told you I could sell the plan.* They stare like they've never seen me before. And they haven't. Not this version. I am missing a chunk of my hair. I am new. Their son is—for a sweet, brief second—a serious businessman. I want to feel pride, but something in their faces makes me sick. *Sold it all. Even the briefcase,* I lie. Everyone says *Bret* as if my name is a rare stone found only in the ocean. But it isn't praise they're giving me. No one notices the money, only the braid, the rope of hair, still knotted with the little green heart.

Mom screams. Dad cackles. Derek disappears. The house collapses.

I awoke from my fantasy in the yard, having made it all the way to our house on the hill.

Walking inside suddenly seemed terrifying, so I stood on tiptoes at the living room window. Mom paced the kitchen, the cordless phone in her butt-pocket. Dad and Derek sat at the table, still dressed in their stupid suits. I wanted Dad to stand up and stop Mom's pacing with a hug, wanted to reach through the window and tap Derek on the shoulder. *Hey, dude, I've got a surprise.* No one spoke. The TV was the only noise—local news, crime.

We'll alert you as soon as we know more, said a reporter. *But we're hearing reports that the victim is a teenaged boy, sixteen, found early this evening in Logan Park.*

Mom rushed into the dining room. "He's got to be out there, you two! Take the car." When Dad and Derek stood up from the table and started putting on their shoes, I tried to knock on the window, but my knuckles just bounced against the screen. I wanted to speak, but all that came out was a cough. The three of them turned toward my sound, staring at the front door in silence, as if it might burst open. I waved behind the window, but they still didn't see me.

It turns out that we do have a true self, something that never changes even when every other part of you has. The true self is what's there when no one you love will look at you.

The TV talked of stab wounds, sirens, victims, suspects, words I didn't decipher. A sick taste climbed my throat. I felt flimsy. This oddness rushed through my body like blood, a sensation I could not have named. Responsibility, guilt—I still feel it now—shame.

I ran to the side yard. Blood sloshed in my head, washing away old cells. New ones grew, snapping like Pop Rocks. I hoped they were good cells—sturdy, dependable. I prayed that they would stay and thrive and be the foundation of the final me. But I could already feel them dying, slipping, snowing through my body like static. I puked so many of them into our garden.

As the men of the family climbed into the station wagon to find me, backing out of the driveway into the night, I hid behind the pepper plants, keeping low to the ground. When the motor's hum died away, the world was totally silent—Mom had turned the TV off—and I heard my heart beating against the dirt. Hand in my pocket, I gripped Kiana's braid.

She would be the one to confess to her mom about what we'd

done. There were so many witnesses to describe me. The lawsuit would come for us, for my parents, for reckless endangerment, and eventually, when all was settled and done, for the house.

I laid in the garden and stared at it, our big house. How had it changed us? How would we be different if we'd kept living down the hill? The day's events must have knocked loose memories, because suddenly I could picture the little slice of a house we used to have, tucked in the middle of that long row, a tiny sliver of that street-length brick building, with the thin walls and the yelling next door, the cats on the porch, the bed I shared with Derek, the dinners without Dad, and the quiet breakfasts while he slept, and the church full of singing neighbors. I was falling asleep, beginning to dream my past life into existence, but then the back door swung open and banged closed.

At the far end of the garden, my mother appeared. She stood still, staring through all of her plants. She didn't see me out there, blending in, growing every second into something none of us understood. But then she moved closer, slowly, stepping through the garden, swimming carefully toward me, until she found my arm and screamed and gripped it so hard she left marks. When she asked me where I'd been, I said I didn't know, and we both knew it was a total lie. I had been here, in my body, this whole time.

THE IDLER

South Dakota stretches out like a cold, brown, made bed. It's been two years, but I still can't find comfort here. And no, I haven't seen the state's more alien places—those Badlands, Black Hills, all crag and moonscape. Mainly I've stayed here, in Pierre. Whose fault? I won't point fingers. Going places makes me nervous. I don't claim to be made for better things, but I can't help talking a little shit on Pierre. My fiancé will sigh, *Did we not make this decision together?*

Locals pronounce it *Peer*, like staring, but I prefer to say it fully French. Sometimes, when I make it to one of his Humanities department parties, I'll even gargle the *r* sound.

I'll even spit a little.

The idler returns during our quiet fight about the future. I'm playing a cell phone game with the sound loud, a swiper called *TAGASSASSIN* where you slice the tags that jut up from people's shirt collars. It's very trying, this game. Casualties abound, and many necks bleed.

It's ten at night, December—a dirty, crisp winter. Earphones in, my fiancé, Corey, reads for his thesis, which was due last month. Move out by Christmas was the plan, but now we'll be here through May. I have not yet told Dad. I wait, slice tags. The dog whines. The idler idles.

The idler's been outside our apartment nearly every night since November. What idles is a fat-ass, cobalt F-250. I think the word for it is *lifted*. Exhaust pumps out via chrome pipes that jut up like devil horns. A rear window decal reads, *This TRUCK Is an Answered Prayer*. Around eight its engine fires, but it goes nowhere, just sits still in the frost, releasing white exhaust, the rattle of its idle seeping through the carpet. I mean, you can literally feel it in your feet.

I pinch the dog's pink rubber chicken from under the couch and whip it in the direction of the kitchen, which, yes, is in the direction of Corey's head. It soars. The dog scrambles.

"Your aim's way off," he says, one earphone popped out.

His thesis is about how no one knows anymore what the divine is. And when he started it, two years ago, he was a hard, true nonbeliever. An atheist with a grudge, and sideburns, like the men in cop dramas. He had that hot confidence only a twenty-two-year-old can love. People praying, the pledge of allegiance, Christmas mangers with actual dead-eyed dolls inside—these things grated on him. He faulted religion for all the world's ills, and in a rush to become the Dick Dawkins of his generation, we whirlwinded out here from Santa Rosa on his first and only offer. But now, he's read so damn much about holiness, ritual, and deep breathing that God enters our talks as often as the dog. It's all we discuss: the dog, the frequency/shape of the dog's shits in freezing temps, and God. Or—*he* talks. I nod. I proof his pages. I do dishes. Listen, it's not like he's Christian. Not even Universalist, yet. We don't do church, but his eyes fix on the stained glass anytime we pass one of the twenty in town. It's all theory at this point, but it scares me—how a place plus enough time can morph a person wholly.

I chuck the chicken again, and it nips his bald spot. Okay, I know I'm more creative than this. My first and only prof—Photography 1 at Napa Valley College—said I had *a wild eye for detail, but no focus*. To think I told Dad I'd be out here taking photos. Photos of?

Ice? Trucks? "The idler's set a record," I say now to Corey. "Two hours straight."

He says: nothing. Recently he said this thing while I cooked our quinoa: *Man is his God*. Meaning, I think, that whatever strikes in us a divine mood—say, the dog's tongue between your toes—those moments are the foundation of one's true, unmalleable self. Or maybe it means nothing. Maybe he still believes that because he's eight years older, everything he says sounds prophetic to my ears. Maybe it did, once. Point is, I should find something new to do—I stew, I swipe, I smoke, I work at Triple Thrift. My Nikon gathers dust above the fridge.

Maybe woman is her boredom. "Did you hear me?" I say.

"I'm concentrating," he says, earphones back in, eyes glued to the Mac's holy glow.

At first, the idler was a blessing. What a thrill it is to have a new topic. Together we'd bitch, theorize, and rail against the idler. *What's the point of sitting in a truck? Is he selling drugs? Global warming, hello? That's bad for the engine, right?* With a subject to reunite us, we were snappy, buzzing, fun. Motherfucking idler. But tonight solidifies the truth. We've gotten to that inevitable point: the idling isn't interesting. We no longer ask the rhetoricals. We don't sing the word *idle* to the tune of pop hits. It's been weeks since we've gotten on our knees at the front window to spy clues, watch the white exhaust slip through the frost. We don't escape to bed together and hide from the sound under the covers, don't wrestle ourselves into a kind of sixty-nine until our hairy legs muff each other's ears. We no longer fuck above the growl of the idle.

The dog grumbles, impersonating the truck. Corey opens another book. It is winter. It is dry, but the engagement ring feels tight around my finger. I slice a tag, make a gash in the nape of an old hag's neck.

My phone battery hits 10 percent. I don't care if it's cliché to be homesick for the Pacific. I miss seeing people barefoot. I'd kiss—no, I'd *lick*—a rock outcropping at Gualala.

I haven't left our place much since my Pap died last winter. He'd lived in my father's house for twelve years. At the funeral I promised Dad (an addict, hippie, widower) that we'd be back in Cali soon. I tucked his drunk ass into bed that night, and we shook hands like a deal.

"I want to leave," I say, though I'm not sure my voice carries above the idle's murmur.

"Huh?" he says. "I thought every time you leave the house you get sick?"

"That's not what I—" but the idler does this thing where he must be juicing the gas. The sound of the idle surges in waves. The warm floor beneath me swells. I'd hold my breath for a month under ocean water. I would. I want to tell him this, but the idle, the idle is scream, and I can't take it anymore, can't hear myself think. So instead what I do is I put on my boots.

I put on my biggest, darkest coat.

From our driveway, the sheer size of the country seems to rise up and flash me. Hulking, huge, it lays bare its breast, as if taunting: *Stab here. Hit heart and anywhere blood runs, you can go.*

This is what we fight about, because now he might stay on for a teaching certificate, might adjunct here next fall. He's not sure, doesn't want to talk about summer. He only wants to talk about *now*. This very moment. As if now is enough. I want answers; he wants us to meditate.

There's nothing exactly wrong with this place: it's our building, and behind that a shuttered Dairy Queen, a beaming gas station called Kwik Stuff. Pierre's eleven thousand people but feels like four. The air is brittle. I step through snow littered with dogshit and cig butts, to the idler.

With my ungloved knuckle I tap the frozen window. The truck's engine surges, but the wheels don't spin. I breathe into my red, raw hands and wait. Okay, so he can idle. And I can play chicken. I'll stand here until the tank's out of gas. I'll drink snow, live off grass. In the distance, I hear a voice crackle through a speaker. A streetlight dies, flickers, holds. I knock again, and the window slides down at a crawl. I can see someone with long blond hair leaning across the cab toward me. She's cranking the window down, manually.

Woman is her hands.

"Help you?" she says, the window now half-mast. It's dark inside the cab—a glowing green stereo the only light. Faintly, I hear a pop song about the answer to all questions being *No.*

"You're idling out here," I say.

"You're observant out here," she says. It's unnerving that I can't make out her face. Mine I'll bet shines in the streetlight beside me. I wonder what that picture looks like.

"I live here," I say. "And the idle, you know, we can hear it clearly."

"A warm noise," she says. "Don't it sound like a soup on boil?"

It does. And there's ice forming on the fine but not unnoticeable hairs of my upper lip.

"Why is it you're always out here," I say, "idling?"

"Waiting for the storm to pass," she says, pointing to a house down street. "Listen."

She kills the engine. First I find a fading voice on the Kwik Stuff loudspeaker, a cashier yelling, *Go ahead pump 3! Pump it up!* Then, it's the rattle of traffic over the Missouri River.

Finally, I hear yelling. I see lights in what must be her house flipping on and off, flares flashing bright like a brain hooked up to a computer and you're watching it think, or sleep.

"Why don't you leave?" I say. "Go somewhere."

"Here works. Plus, who's got gas money?" The wind blows into my ear. I shift weight to feel my toes. "So, you just gonna stand there and freeze?" she says. "It's unlocked."

I sense a face in the window behind me, watching as I climb into shotgun. The song plays, and I sit, idle. I wonder how I'm here. And why. I feel anxious, like I might puke. Then I look—the face in the window is the dog's. All that snout fog. It doesn't show, but she's an ancient, regal breed, companion of choice for Egyptian queens.

"I got gas money," I say, reaching for my wallet. "Gin money, too."

On the thirty-second drive from our block to the Kwik Stuff, I learn her name—"Ka*reen*, like when the car goes off the cliff"—and, thanks to the glare of the red light on her crow's feet, I learn that she might be fifteen, twenty years my senior. "I'm Blair," I tell her. "I live here." And I motion to the gas station, trying to add a little laugh. The last time I went out, over a month ago now, I left the grad student soiree halfway through, took our Civic home alone, my coat covering the passenger seat like a tarp for my climbing vomit. I don't know what it is, this dizziness that's been hitting me each time I leave the house. Triple Thrift has no health plan.

But here, with the idler, I feel strangely fine, even hungry.

"What's your name mean?" I ask. "Like, how'd you get it?"

"Oh no," she says. "You don't get off on talking about the past, do you?"

Half the *U* is out on the sign, so it looks like Kwik Stiff. We pull up to a pump where a taped paper sign says *No CARDS*, but then the next pump says, *Not HERE either*, so we hop out of the truck.

"You ever meet the kid in here?" Kareen says as we approach the shop, and for some reason I look to see if she's pointing at her torso. The child inside.

But I remember him as soon as we enter the store.

"Ladies!" he says, holding a spent lotto card. "Did I just win the frickin' jackpot?"

Julio is five foot nothing with a smooth, greasy face and exhausted eyes. You could guess him anywhere between age sixteen and thirty-six. The southern accent might be affected. He's the night manager, which on a Tuesday means he's the only one in the store, and he just has a blast. You have to love that, and I do, somewhere, but it's this thing that happens even with my happy lady coworkers—their snappy energy seems to sap mine. It feels like a challenge, a taunt, a brag. "Anything at all," he says as Kareen picks an aisle. "My employee discount is yours."

Once, in Corey's first semester here, I came to the Kwik Stuff stinking of reefer to raid the taquito rollers. Julio was behind the register dribbling a basketball painted to look like Earth. At checkout he took the bag full of scabby taco-hot dogs from my hand, leaned across the counter, and whispered, "Ma'am, if you wait here six minutes, I'll make you four of these fresh." He gave me a chair. We talked about our favorite highways. He asked if I had seen him in the local Kwik Stuff commercial, said he hates *the idea* of Hollywood but he's saving up anyway.

At the counter now, I tell him to give me twenty on Pump Three. He salutes me, rounds the counter, pushes out the doors, jogs over to the pumps, drops down on the ground bright with frost, and starts doing push-ups. His breath against the concrete makes a cloud around his head. After Kareen quits laughing, it gets quiet.

You can hear him out there, counting each one out. She reaches over the counter, steers the bendy mic toward her face and says, "Enough already, Jules. We got drunk to go get." When he comes back through the door, panting and smiling like a dog, we clap. He rings up Kareen's Doritos and my pack of gum, puts the money on the pump.

"Your nametag's spelled wrong," I tell him, maybe rubbing it in. "It says *manger*."

"That's because I'm the manger," Julio says. He frowns when I don't laugh.

Kareen leans forward. "That mean you have a baby inside you?" Their laughter is stupid loud. I wish she wouldn't, but Kareen tells Julio to meet us at Skiv's when he's off. He gives two thumbs-up. We leave with the bell above the door jingling. In the parking lot, I turn back to our apartment's kitchen window, which you can see above the Kwik Stuff roof. My fiancé washes a dish, his eyes sinkward, lips moving like he's singing, praying, or maybe cursing my name.

"Why'd you get so much gas?" Kareen says, climbing into shot-gun. "Skiv's is a mile."

She's left the keys on the hood, for me.

The drive to Skiv's Bar & Off Sale is quick. Behind the wheel, I take it in. Dad taught me to drive stick when I was fifteen so I could be his and Pap's ride home from the Legion. Pap—my mother's dad—moved in with us after she passed in '04. He and Dad were like shitty big brothers through my adolescence, chock full of advice and bluster, but with zero will to cook or clean the house. I kept order. I drove them home to pristine beds, sheets tucked tight so no one would roll off to the floor. I wonder who does this for Dad now—or does he have a bed at the bar?

On Sioux Avenue we pass a man in a snowsuit with a trash bag slung over his shoulder.

"I didn't know a town this small could have homeless," I say.

"Oh, yeah," Kareen says. "Everywhere." In the side mirror we get a look at how big and gray and frostbitten his beard is, and he looks just like my Pap. It's a red light, so I pull out my phone. I ignore the missed calls, open the camera. The last pic on here is from months ago, Corey holding a journal he had a paper in. I'd sent it to Dad, no reply. Turns out, the blurry photo I take of the man at the corner is artistically/morally fucked. My phone dies in protest.

"Feel like I should pull over and bring him to the bar too," I say, a little bitter and annoyed she invited Julio, nervous he'll burst into Skiv's smelling like hot dogs and gas, demanding us to dance. "I could just collect *all* the town misfits, deliver them to sanctuary."

"Wait," Kareen says. "If anyone's the collector, it's me. Whose truck you think this is?"

Skiv's is nothing special. Is anything? The taps total two, the pool tables are so unlevel your beer slides down the runner, and the bathroom's all puddles. But it feels like the Legion out in Windsor where Dad and Pap would eat broasted chicken, pound Coors, fight over the video bingo, and then call. I won't say Skiv's is like home. But it's something. It's a deep breath.

Kareen and I pick a wobbly high-top. Behind the bar, Skiv shakes an alarm clock like a piggy bank. He's Lakota. Oglala, I think. His front teeth are chipped like the sharp edge of a key. "I'm no delivery boy," he says, pointing to our drinks, so Kareen goes and grabs them.

It's five quiet men at the bar, and one other lonely table—graduate students by the looks of them. They don't make a peep, seem sad, just sitting there like the cursed sons of Abraham.

"To making our husbands worry," I say, raising my gin to meet Kareen's Bud.

"Oh honey," Kareen says to me in a tone too motherly. "That ain't my man."

"Well then who was that . . . storm?"

"That's my *old* man."

Three years ago she moved here from Fargo to see him through his dementia after he'd been ejected from a nursing home for stabbing an orderly with a fork. She's got two brothers but neither offered to move home. Anyway, Kareen was always the favorite. "Meaning, I'm the only one he never hit," she says. "The brother whose truck we're driving—he's been visiting for a bit, his first time here in two years, but now all the sudden he's leaving before Christmas. Can't hack it." She spits in a napkin. "I don't want to talk about this. To answer your question: no husband."

We both take gulps. "Me either," I say. "Not yet, at least." I hold up my hand, show my subtle ring. It's exactly the one I wanted, and I received it exactly when I thought I wanted it, and I even like the look of it still. But two years in, this thing has disappeared into my hand, another part of myself I forget about, like a useless extra knuckle—so why do I take it off?

When I hand it to Kareen. she feels the band like it's silk. A long time she holds my ring, gently, like it's a tiny animal, and I don't know why I'm expecting her to, but she never tries it on. Behind the bar, Skiv flicks the small, blinking alarm clock with his middle finger. "Where'd the time go?" he keeps saying to its face. "Piece of shit. You had *one* job."

When Kareen hands the ring back, I don't put it where it belongs. I set it on a napkin.

"I'll give you ten dollars for it," she says, laughing. We listen to Tom Petty croon.

"Fuck it. Let's go to the Badlands tonight," I say.

"Absolutely," Kareen says, knocking back her pint and heading to the restroom. "Not."

I follow her in, keep my eyes from the mirror. There's nothing wrong with forsaking make-up, but I hate to be reminded of things I've forgotten. I try to picture my ring on the table.

"So, never?" I say. "No marriage for you?"

"Eh, once," Kareen says from the stall. "It was—we had a good one, far as marriages go. You know, if there's such a thing as a good one. Which, yeah, you know. Well, there ain't."

"What happened? Boredom? Disrespect? He a drunk?" I can feel the sweet gin squeezing the back of my brain. "He fuck the milkman? You still have them around here, right?"

"Tell me you're not one of these women who wants to get away from certain things just to go someplace else and bitch about the things she left," she says, emerging from the stall.

When he asked me to leave California with him, I was just learning to surf. I'd wanted to do it forever, had finally started, had even saved up for a camera you strap to your head. I was taking stills from those films, making a kind of collage. My then-boyfriend loved it. Ironically he used the words *sublime*, *divine*. We were in love. He showed me the first chapter of his book. I flipped through it, so proud, but never read a word. I trusted him. He got into grad school—he got us here. We got engaged. I followed him, thinking maybe I'd be his photographer, archivist, sounding board, treasurer, chef, wife, distraction—but what I became was nothing.

"This place isn't all that bad," I say to Skiv. Kareen's gone out to smoke in the cold, so I'm alone at the table, swirling the melted ice in my glass. "Still, you couldn't pay me to stay."

"Important to remember: most of us didn't *choose* to live here," he says.

"Point taken," I say, toasting no one. "Dude, will you take me to the Badlands?"

"Welcome," he says, and pushes into the kitchen.

As I was leaving the apartment tonight, there came a moment where I almost turned around. At the bottom of our stairs stood the door—ice had not only grown on the inside of the windows, which I have seen before, but it'd crawled through the knob, spread across the wood panels, and the whole door was one slab of crusted cold. When I wrenched the deadbolt to open, the squealing, nail-on-glass sound made my teeth ache. I thought I was trapped. But I acted. An impulse to confront the truck had led me to the foot of the stairs, and a weird fear of frost was not going to stop me. I opened the door. Impulse is a place. Maybe that's what here is.

So, I do it again. I get up and head for the table of grad students, all of them looking sleepy. They wear those hats with the flaps that hide your ears, but none of them fit.

"Any of you know my husband, Corey? Corey Westerling?"

"Uh," says the group's one woman, her glasses foggy from a hot cider. "The God guy?"

"Yes," I say, putting a hand on her shoulder. "Can you convince him not to stay?"

"Stay? Wait, why would he stay here?"

"In this backwoods shithole?" says a guy with an accent I can't place.

"Well," I say. "I wouldn't call it that."

"Don't they have God everywhere?" says the woman, and then the door behind me opens with a frost we all feel instantly. Kareen comes over, puts a hand on my shoulder to collect me. We regain our table, get more drinks, and become the talk of the grad student booth.

"Okay, so let me try another," I say.

"Jesus," Kareen says. "We're back to twenty questions?" The neon digital jukebox by the door comes alive with Queen.

"You think anything's holy?"

"Not anything," she says and drains half her glass. "But most of it."

I end up pouring a lot on Kareen—the coast, his thesis, my dog, anxiety, my dad, his dad. Though the paper said *natural causes*, it was an overdose with Pap, his pain pills—I think they were crushing them up. Dad denies it, but he does them too. Kareen's not asking for any of this, and she doesn't pretend to like it, but she listens, nods. Mom was gone before I knew what guidance was. At this point, I'd try a psychic. I'd read tea leaves. I'd take notes from God.

"Okay, okay," Kareen says. "I don't know why you look at me and think, *she's* got advice. But, a diagnosis: If you run back to the west, won't it just be taking care of a different man? Your father's an adult. Anyway, seems all the same to me—here, there."

In order not to bawl, I turn my head to the back of the bar, and how did I not notice this before? On the dance floor stand eight Christmas trees, each decorated by a different local Business-of-Promise, and you're supposed to vote. My money's on the Vacuum Repair spruce, all wrapped in tubes, ornaments made from mangled coins, combs, a little Lego cowboy hat. The travel agency's one is cerulean—is that spray paint?—like they were going for ocean but missed.

Kareen asks Skiv what the winner gets.

"A bar."

Kareen laughs, and I try, I really do try to join her, but still it doesn't take.

✳

At midnight Julio comes through the door in a gust of wind. "You ladies look El Niño drunk."

Kareen shrugs, "We give up."

"Kind of drunk only comes once every *seven* years." And I want to blink his happy face away, but he turns it to me. "I feel like the world's worst neighbor—I never got your name."

"Blair," I say, "like the witch."

"Wait a second," he says. "Turn around." And I don't know why, but I do. He touches the top of my shirt, and he's about a foot shorter than me, so I imagine him back there, reaching up like a sapling. "Your tag is out," he says, flipping it down into my shirt collar.

I spin around to face him like he called me a name. "So what?" I say, embarrassed.

"Just what I thought," he says, grinning down into his shirt collar. "Made in heaven."

For the first time in this time zone, I laugh without trying. Somebody puts a rap song on, the one about the windows and the wall, and everybody's on their feet, even the students, and we each pick a gaudy pine to dance beside. My laughter becomes constant and rushing, like a thaw shaking awake a creek. I catch my reflection in the one unfogged window near the bathroom—I'm a tree full of holes and light.

I'll leave. It's what happens. But first, I'll forget my ring on the table, have Kareen haul me home, where Corey and the dog are in a panic and I'll plead with him, *Drive us to the Badlands*, tell him I'm fixed, I can go places, I'm fine, I love you, I'm ready, it's 1:00 a.m., but let's go to a national park and watch the sunrise, we won't take pictures, we'll enjoy it in the moment, we'll say a mantra, I can do this, I can savor things now, I want to discuss who runs the world, and eventually I'll wear him down, we'll even get the dog in the car, he'll start the engine, and with my hands on my head, he'll see it, my naked finger, and he'll break the silence with sobs, and he'll march back inside, hysterical, because some things are sacred. He'll leave me with the dog, lights beaming, keys in the ignition, the future. I'll get all the practice I need to leave him, my family, my self. I take the wheel. First I drive to Skiv's, and it's waiting beneath an overturned pint glass, like the ring is a roach. I put it in my pocket, leave, head south, stop at Get&Go to puke and ask the rude attendant what a Badland is, and if the sun really rises over those hills of perfect dirt, pink-gold spires, bison, a moon landing, a cleaving—I end up on an empty road, squinting into darkness through the open window, seeing nothing, but knowing full well it's all here.

MS. BADISLAV'S VOMIT

Our church had a drive-thru window.

It was meant for those who couldn't make the service, who couldn't take another night like the one they'd had before—those disgruntled and hungry few who, wishing the squat blue building was still a Hardee's, drove through just to air their grievances. The window, its glass permanently stained with bird shit, was open all weekend long.

And one Sunday morning, beneath that open window, we found Pastor Christine hog-tied, asleep on the floor. Our donation box, gone. The pastor was fine, physically, and insisted on delivering her sermon, in which she declared that if you're looking for God—even in the ski-masked face of an attacker—you will see God.

Example A: she told the attacker she'd pray for him, and he thanked her.

Example B: she spoke of the robins that had flown in during the early morning hours and started a nest in the old soda fountain behind our altar. The birds had even used our church merch—threads from our cotton tees, bits of our Now Is a Gift That's Why They Call It the Present bumper stickers—in the weaving of their home. No one asked for evidence to back these crazy claims. When she got on a roll, reality itself seemed to hover just above the ground.

"These creatures came to us," she preached. "We've made a sanctuary."

It was a tough sell, convincing us the burglary was a feature, not a bug, of our community outreach project.

"Listen, Chris, can we close the damn drive-thru already?" someone said from a corner booth. (Most tables hadn't been converted yet to pews, the bulk of our funds having been spent to paint the puke-blue walls white). "It's unsafe. Plus unpopular." The speaker, Ms. Badislav, was my agitated psych teacher who seemed to hate our church yet attended every week, someone with whom, I noticed, our fearless pastor never made eye contact. "Let's give it up."

The twenty-person congregation groaned in agreement, the noise echoing off the plastic order boards still mounted to the walls. But Pastor Christine was adamant about staying open. She said the night spent on the floor of the vestibule had been humbling, that she'd heard God whistling "through the window of her dreams." In fact, she wanted the drive-thru operational every night of the God-given week—"Yes, starting tomorrow"—and were there any volunteers?

"Come on, people," she said, stomping. "Communities don't make themselves!"

So I stood up. The congregants gasped. I needed community service hours in order to graduate. Yes, there was the fact that I hated people, almost everyone, especially the locals of Deliver, a place voted number three in Pennsylvania's Top Small Towns to Leave. I went to church mainly to get away from my family, to feel sullen before the epic grace of God, who I did not believe in, but had always secretly wished to reach, like the unbeatable boss at the end of an RPG. A popular school-wide joke was that I'd be nominated Most Likely to Shoot the Place Up.

But there was also a chance my father (long ago a faithful member) might stop by to pray forgiveness, maybe lecture me about all the data I was using to watch porn on my smartphone. He'd left a month ago in the middle of an ugly fight with Mom where, to underscore a point, he put a pair of hedge clippers through our aboveground pool, flooding the patio so bad that water dripped from the ceiling of my basement bedroom.

Our church—though recently robbed, suffering from low attendance, inhabited by eccentrics and birds—was one of the more stable institutions in my life.

Pastor Christine shook my hand hard and then called for a round of applause.

That Monday, Pastor Christine coached me through my first shift. She'd cut her hair off and looked a bit like Alice from *Resident Evil*, but with braces. Her hands shook, so she sat on them. "Most people who stop by are just curious. Offer basic info on the church—service times, dates for the barbeque. Don't get bogged down in scripture and interpretation of rules. Don't debate the half-baked philosophy majors. Some people will want to pray, and that's what it's all about. Remember: focus on gratitude, not desire."

"And what about the people who want to rob us?"

She was silent, staring out at the dark, empty parking lot. "Just give," she said, eventually. "Give whatever they ask for."

With my pastor beside me I couldn't watch porn, so I passed the hours searching her Bible for its more cinematic moments—floods, miracles, cities destroyed—but all I kept finding were the lists of names, the begetting and begotten. The only person to stop by was an old man who didn't know how to roll his window down and yelled through the glass that he wanted a roast beef and two Cokes, and one of the Cokes, goddamnit, was a Dr Pepper. I waved a brochure at him, pantomimed prayer. He gave me the finger and left.

"Just think, Pierce," the pastor said, handing me a church key so I could let myself in the next night. "This will make the perfect college admission essay."

I think we both knew that I would never apply to college. But what neither of us knew was how I'd stagger into adulthood like a slow crash, burn for a decade, see my own death reflected in the eye of a wild ocean, and finally return to work as a custodian for the now thriving, expanded First Community Church of Deliver (by that time housed in a converted bus depot, with seating for three hundred, and no plastic booths crusted to hell with stuck gum). In fact, I'm glad neither of us saw this coming. Life should be lived in providence, not prophecy.

At home that night, my mother was in my bedroom, poking at the growing green spot in the corner of my ceiling. The pool water was seeping in and my room smelled like Clorox and semen. "You know what this means?" she said, touching the swampy ceiling tile. Mom taught English lit in the next county over and lived by the metaphor of everything. I was tired, depressed about the Roast Beef & Dr Pepper guy, and just wanted to masturbate myself to sleep. I looked out the window, checked the backyard for my father's truck. "I think it means you were overchlorinating the pool."

"It's the void, love. It seeks us out. It always meets us exactly where we are." She went on as I fell asleep, the it she rambled about sounding a lot like Pastor Christine's idea of God.

Most of the next night's window shift I spent bored on my phone, surfing porn, openly inviting God not to speak to me. I'd watched so much that I needed videos revolving around improbable and physically uncomfortable scenarios, like, for example, there's an exercise ball between them. Or a housewife, having knocked a fresh pie off a low windowsill, leans out the window to retrieve it, and the window falls closed, and for some reason she's stuck there, pinned at the waist, and then a man comes in, like her boyfriend or the gas guy, and he teases her about the situation, offers to help if he can take her. And with little debate she agrees. And then they do it, her top half-clothed and kind of rocking out the window, but inside, her skirt's hiked up and her legs wobble from the awkwardness of the position. I liked to imagine that after it was over they'd eat the pie together in the kitchen, not bothering to pick the blades of grass or pieces of mulch out of the filling, just eating and smiling, naked, like it all made sense. But I never got to the end.

I'd been watching one of those videos when the night's first car pulled up to the window.

"You about bored?" Ms. Badislav said, idling. She had a curly black ball of hair, sharp blue eyes, and a mole on her cheek that looked like a piece of Cookie Crisp cereal. She taught Psychology & Economics, which was for some reason a single class. Maslow's hierarchy, id and ego, the archetypes of dreams—this was her Monday-Wednesday-Friday. But Tuesday-Thursday was supply and demand, inflation, a Wall Street simulation game called Mock Market. No matter what day of the week, when you walked into Ms. Badislav's room, Tracy Chapman's "Fast Car" blasted from her laptop. Besides that, she was totally unpredictable, shouty and bitter in lectures, and often late to class. Twice she'd cancelled tests to show us her taped-from-TV copy of *Sunday Bloody Sunday* while she plucked nose hairs, using her webcam as a mirror.

She honked her car's weak horn at me.

"I'm fine," I said, sliding my phone under a Bible on the counter, an unsmooth move I used in her class often. "It's pretty chill here, kinda meditative. Just sitting, looking out."

"At this beautiful parking lot," she said. "And that rusted fence over there. Very tranquil. Nothing screams Zen like broken beer bottles and No Loitering signs."

I laughed. Was this flirting? The closest I had come to flirting was giving this androgynous night elf all my rare swords in *World of Warcraft*. I leaned forward in my chair, my head a little out the window, and noticed her eyes were bloodshot as shit.

"What?" she said. "You see the devil in me?"

"No, I—"

"Is Chris even here?"

"Just me," I said. "Pastor Christine is taking a hiatus from the drive-thru, considering—"

"If I ever find the motherfucker," Ms. Badislav said, but she looked disappointed. Her car—a junky sky-colored Camry from the early nineties—rattled harshly, the ceiling liner drooping onto her head. I heard the snap-hiss of a can opening. Ms. Badislav brought a Yuengling to her lips and turned her stereo up. Tracy Chapman's low, smoky voice was unmistakable. *You and I can both get jobs. And finally see what it means to be living.* She handed the can out of her window. I believe now that this night was the closest I ever came to God. But at seventeen, sitting in the drive-thru of my church, I just thought this woman was into me.

"I can't," I said, thinking of Mom pumping my father's entire beer keg down the tub the day he stabbed the pool and left, how she'd tossed the empty drum down the wooded hill of our backyard, how I'd counted the black birds that escaped into the sky. Twenty-one.

"Huh," she said. "Chris always trades sips when she prays with me."

I reached through the open window, and she put the can in my hand. The first sip tasted like wet wood. As I leaned out to hand it back, I took a long look around the parking lot for my father's truck. The place was empty. He was never coming. He would never be watching. I took another sip. "What do you two pray about?" I said.

"Everything," she said. "Opposite things. Like Chris prays for her teeth to finally turn straight. And I pray she never takes those braces off because I love the way they cut up my tongue. And Chris prays the church will survive the downturn. I pray she leaves her husband, and I pray for more beer, and she prays for forgiveness for the ones we've emptied. She prays for the world to disarm and join hands. I pray for an explosion we can watch from the rearview on the interstate, the windows all down, hands clasped together on the gearshift. Am I too poetic?" I pictured her face, taut and red in the grip of lecture. I thought of her and Pastor Christine together, their secret, sacred community of two, and I tried to act unsurprised, cool, and detached, like a man who enters a kitchen to find a woman in the window. "Poetic?" I said.

"In class, do I sound like a hippie? A bitter hippie. Is that how I come off?"

"You come off, like, psych and econ are just horrible games rich men play, like golf."

She opened the car door, planted her hands on the drive-thru windowsill, and said, "That's the nicest thing anyone has ever said to me." She hoisted herself up, bent at the waist, and yelled, "Man overboard!" as she tumbled face first into the church, kicking the shelf above the window. An old box of straws rained down onto our heads. I gave her space. I sat on the floor.

For the rest of my second night at the window, I watched Ms. Badislav command the drive-thru. I took notes, drinking my half of every Yuengling. It seemed as if her very presence in that office chair brought people to us. We stayed open well past midnight. Eight cars came in total, and at one point, there was a short line. Every person that pulled up, part of me wanted them to leave. What did we have to offer to anyone? But Ms. Badislav never blinked. She stayed motivated. In the face of so much nothing, she chose to respond, her voice at times reaching its sweet spot—that zealous, happy shouting. It was an hours-long communion.

"If you want to split hairs," she said, "*breathing* is hope."

"It's too easy . . . it's too *boring* not to have faith," she said.

"If there's even a question," she said, "then you quit that fucking job!"

Without her, there, that night, I don't think I would've ever been able to look at a person and see through to their community. Community as an inherent object. An invisible, internal human organ, like a soul, but with arms reaching out. Beside her I felt seen, and grown, but not even a touch less terrified. Weeks later my father would pull up to my window, and, trembling, I'd convince him to cook the scrambled eggs for the annual pancake breakfast. I'd make him promise to use a little milk in the recipe. I remember he brought his own wok.

At two in the morning Ms. Badislav puked on the floor, and before I ran off to try to find a mop, I thought I saw something in the yellow vomit. I convinced myself it was nothing, only what my mother always saw: the big, vague void. When I came back with a stack of napkins, Ms. Badislav was gone, but the vomit was still there, and the church was so filled with the odor of yeast, you could smell something growing.

I looked again at the puke, at the image it was now undoubtedly making. A circle. A face, but blank. A clock with both hands stuck. The building's foundation wasn't level, because the vomit was running, moving, though time was not, and I stepped out of the way as the clock morphed into a boat, and it sailed, and the hands of the clock broke into pieces, now people on the deck, so many people, waving as they left on the waves of a great flood, and I waved back until I saw that they were climbing the mast, until they were all crowded together in the crow's nest, until I saw that I was one of them.

SPIRITUAL INTRODUCTION TO THE NEIGHBORHOOD

Claw Street

One once witnessed, in the quick dark of an autumn night, two youths coming down Claw on skateboards, holding hockey sticks against the asphalt, producing startling orange sparks. Idling at the stop sign, one watched and worried as the pair tore downhill at speeds in the neighborhood of twenty miles per hour. The skaters reached the intersection, veering to flank one's Honda. Somewhere, barking dogs hushed. Sometimes one must close one's eyes and let the world pass by, is the advice here, though this (one swears) is not that type of literature. The youths, thank heaven, simply kept cruising. From the rearview mirror, their sparks resembled long, ignited leads running to a single pile of dynamite in the distance.

That, or stars fallen into town.

Prushing Street

Here, in this divot on the Minnesota River valley, resides a gray squirrel with half a tail who thinks it's whole. Sipping morning tea, one might witness her—tail no longer than a flosser—attempt to leap from a power line to a shed roof and miss. She's lived here fifteen years, well past the average rodent life expectancy. Understand: what's average does not apply here. Every season is wind. Welcome.

ༀ

Watch. Listen, one need not live here for over fifty years in order to see something sacred.

It can happen any moment.

Brunt Way

A stand of bamboo grows all along this lane. One may admire it but mustn't ever enter. Through the shoots sits a farmhouse owned by a childless couple who, rumors say, use the grass in perverse ways. Split down the center, oven-warmed to bake in give, they take the branches to their bedroom. On quiet nights one might hear hot wood striking flesh, the pleasure cries, the keening for God. It is a feat to find sleep here.

It comes from so far away.

Kroll Circle

Here lies the headquarters for Tails of Mending, the dog foster service owned and operated by neighborhood royalty, Jack and Reba Mondell. One might find one's house one day more or less empty and wish for the company of a canine. Say one's partner, long allergic to animals, has passed from a disease no doctor can pronounce. One might telephone Tails of Mending and ask to meet a dog. A shivering Chihuahua. At Triangle Park. As swinging children call out insults—*Taco Bell! Taco Bitch!*—one might fall in love with something so fearful and delicate, with whiskers longer than her very head. One might abide the mandatory home inspection T of M provides to ensure that an adopter's domicile is secure, clean, and absent any signs of mania that might inhibit a mending pet's flourishing. One might feel as though this needless visit has gone swimmingly, ending with a warm handshake and Jack's promise of an email. Could it be that all life requires is a witness? Another pair of eyes nearby and aware. Maybe one's hopes heighten, but that email never comes. One might lay awake nights, listening to the tantra of bruising flesh, wondering what one's error was. One might, weeks later, see the same mending Chihuahua defecate on a tulip at the corner of Claw. One might call and call the headquarters on Kroll. Or show up with fists balled. Jack might deliver some tired version of "it's not you, it's me," where one has been judged "likely to be unfulfilled" by the company of a Chihuahua. One should not cry. One should not buy new furniture, or recaulk the bathtub twice. Return the size extra-small Ultra-Paws Durable Dog Boots to Petco. One does not, honestly, know what one should do. Try writing a cautionary review?

Or a breathing exercise?

Griffin and Andomar Avenues

Here one finds two kinds of yard signs. The first—green, blue, orange—bears the same message in three languages, the gist of which: *all are welcome; love your neighbors.* It's a good sign, though a bit proud—never easy to land square on the side of morality without a touch of peacockishness. A plethora of these exist down Griffin. However, on the parallel Andomar, a different sign is king— Smile, You're on Camera. Passing these properties, one might smile, convinced the snide sign itself is the home's only security system. One might want a jaunt around the block. One might don the New Balance. One might, feeling phlegmy, expectorate on their flowers. Or walk a dog down Andomar, having—oops!—forgotten a bag.

That is, if one has been deemed worthy of a dog.

✳

Kole, Ciara, Xavier

Rarely, one's children might visit. Maybe they sit down on the couch, coats on, to denigrate one's neighborhood. Maybe they're adopted. Maybe they use *bumfuck* in their descriptions. They've come to argue for a move, "the next stage," a home. One might defend this place as home. One might storm out, take a drive, if one's license is not, say, currently wrapped in bureaucratic tape after a brief, victimless incident with a low stone wall on Kroll. Or, one might simply tune the kids out . . . *Adrenoleukodystrophy. Are Jack and Reba homophobes? A-dre-no-leu-ko-dys-tro-phy. The Chihuahua is an ancient, regal breed, the companion of Incan royalty.*

"Wait," the kids might ask, "is this a new couch?"

Sine Qua Non

This is a designation the French use to mean: without which, there is none. *The essential ingredient.* Say, a chili with no tomato. A manhattan sans whiskey. An armless hug. One might live here for decades before questioning what it is that, without it, there is no neighborhood. Is it houses? Humans? Can there *be* a "neighborhood" of only flora and fauna? Do Missing posters nailed to dogwoods a community make? Is it squirrels, failing? Men on disability smoking outside the efficiencies? Gum stuck to sidewalk? Roots breaking asphalt? Cats peering from blinds slats? Bottle shards in the street past closing time?

What is it that, suddenly absent, makes the word *neighborhood* wrong?

Viewpoint

One once used the collective *we* in correspondence. The plural, *us.* But at some point—maybe it was after, say, Jack and Reba's string-pulling resulted in one's removal from the board of Lifelong Learners; or after one's fall outside Triangle Park, when children laughed and no parent looked up from a phone to help; or after witnessing two grown men wielding bamboo stalks like swords in the center of State Street, beating each other to blood—the plural began to feel false. Or was it after the funeral? Is it possible one knows this place not at all?

And so: we fell away to one.

Little Free Libraries #40384 & #40399

Library '84, on Locust, is by a lot the superior repository for literature. There, one finds Twain. One finds Baldwin. One certainly does not find the Cussler, the Evanovich, and the *Idiot's Guide to Home Security* of mid-block Andomar. Feel free to deposit donations in either, but know both are meticulously curated and one's donation may be removed swiftly. (One once gave *Candide* at eight a.m. only to find, on one's fourth walk of the morning, the book gone by nine.) Either that, or one's donations are snatched, devoured, and absorbed by the neighborhood's bibliophilic horde. One might give Vonnegut. Cisneros. Erdrich. One might give *Siddhartha*, twice. One might leave a journal full of personal musings and verse. One might, having given up, give one's letters, scraps. Give everything.

And here, one might find an audience.

ACKNOWLEDGMENTS

The author would like to thank the publications where the following stories previously appeared:

"Once Nothing, Twice Shatter": *The Iowa Review*; a *Best American Short Stories 2020* Distinguished Story

"The Skins": *CRAFT*; *Best Small Fictions* 2020, edited by Nathan Leslie and Elena Stiehler (Sonder Press, 2020)

"Iowa Darter": *Bat City Review*

"Hiccups Forever": *Timber*

"Breakthrough Mailboxes of Southern Pennsylvania": *Subtropics*

"Watchperson": *Heavy Feather Review*

"Eternal Night at the Nature Museum, a Half-Hour Downriver from Three Mile Island": *Passages North*

"Stay, Go": *Gulf Coast*

"Spit If You Call It Fear": *Cream City Review*

"Seven Corners, Pennsylvania—": *The Common*

"Black Sands": *Arcturus*, originally titled "The Orbit of Us"

"K,": *Waxwing*

"Cowboy Man, Major Player": *Many Loops*

"Of a Whole Body (Passing Through)": *Necessary Fiction*

"Midtown": *Best Buds*

"Where the Rubies Live": *Philadelphia Stories*

"The Idler": *Phoebe*

"Ms. Badislav's Vomit": *Outlook Spring*

"Spiritual Introduction to the Neighborhood": *Kenyon Review*

GRATITUDE

Special thanks to the magazine editors who helped make these stories better: Sara Cutaia, Lacey N. Dunham and Steve Himmer, Emily Everett, Molly Gutman, Leah Hampton, Katelyn Keating, David Leavitt, Alex McElroy, Melissa Mesku, Amanda Miska, Andrew Mitchell, Mitchell Sommers, Erin Stalcup and W. Todd Kaneko.

Special thanks to the teachers, peers, and friends who helped make these stories better: Erin Dorney, Pete Stevens, Kaitlyn Andrews-Rice, Dennis Herbert, Michael Torres, James Figy, Robin Becker, Roger Sheffer, Geoff Herbach, Chris McCormick, Bud Smith, and Elle Nash.

This book took its final form at the 2018 Anne LaBastille Memorial Writers Residency. All my gratitude to the Adirondack Center for Writing, Nathalie Thill, Baylee Annis, and the estate of Anne LaBastille.

Lastly, this would not have happened without Kristen Miller and her belief in this book. Your thoughtful revisions, ideas, and guidance have pushed this book closer to perfect. Thank you.

In the past year, I have had many "I wouldn't be a writer if it weren't for _____" moments. That blank space is filled with names of people who supported, encouraged, and loved me, who never turned their noses up when I confessed my dream of writing books—thank you Mom, Dad, Jenna, Barb, Jay, Pat, Deb. These stories are also filled with influences and inspirations that have made me see the world differently—thank you to *Seinfeld*, Lemony Snicket, *Jackass*, Kurt Vonnegut, Adult Swim, Josh Scogin, MF DOOM, Dave Eggers, Mary Ruefle, billy woods, Paul Thomas Anderson, Yayoi Kusama, Lorrie Moore, Isaac Brock, Kathleen Stewart, Rory Allen Philip Ferreira, and I guess I'll stop there. That blank space, which is so full it's breaking the sentence, also includes my teachers and mentors—thank you, Cassi Ney, Barbara Lomenzo, Christine Lincoln, Rick Robbins, Barbara Strasko, Jenny Hill, Barbara DeCesare, and Libby Modern. Lastly, there are places in that space—thank you, Dover, PA; Millersville University; Lancaster, PA; Hamlin, NY; Minnesota State University, Mankato; and the following coffee shops: Javateas, the George Street Cafe, Chestnut Hill Cafe, Square One Coffee, Prince Street Cafe, the Rabbit & the Dragonfly, the Coffee Hag, the Fillin' Station, Java Junction, Copper Cup, and the Blue Line Cafe.

Lastly, to the person who has filled that blank space daily for the past seven years: Erin Dorney. I love you. And Petey too, yes, obviously—but mostly you, Erin.

NOTES

"You've got to be somebody before you can be nobody," from "Once Nothing Twice Shatter," is an adapted Ram Dass aphorism.

The speech quoted in "Once Nothing Twice Shatter" refers to a scene in the 2000 film *Remember the Titans*, written by Gregory Allen Howard and directed by Boaz Yakin (Walt Disney Pictures, Jerry Bruckheimer Films, Technical Black Films).

"Of a Whole Body (Passing Through)" is dedicated to the writers and residents of Assisted Living at Pathstone Crossing in Mankato, Minnesota. Though the vignettes in that story are fictional, I was completely inspired by the energy and honesty of that place. I thank Diana Joseph, Leah Keyes-Hugeback, and Wilbur Neushwander-Frink for the opportunity to volunteer there, as it taught me more about community than anything has.

"Cowboy Dan, Major Player" contains at least a dozen early Modest Mouse references. If you find them all and email me, there's a reward. I'll literally mail you a chapbook or something—I'm serious. Special thanks to Melissa Mesku for prompting this piece.

SARABANDE BOOKS is a nonprofit literary press located in Louisville, KY. Founded in 1994 to champion poetry, short fiction, and essay, we are committed to creating lasting editions that honor exceptional writing. For more information, please visit sarabandebooks.org.